WHAT BOOKS PRESS

AN IMPRINT OF

THE GLASS TABLE

COLLECTIVE

LOS ANGELES

ALSO BY ANDREW TONKOVICH

Orange County: A Literary Field Guide (co-editor, with Lisa Alvarez)
The Dairy of Anne Frank and More Wish Fulfillment in the Noughties

KEEPING TAHOE BLUE AND OTHER PROVOCATIONS

ANDREW TONKOVICH

WHAT
BOOKS
PRESS

LOS ANGELES

Library of Congress Cataloging-in-Publication Data

Names: Tonkovich, Andrew, author.
Title: Keeping Tahoe blue and other provocations / Andrew Tonkovich.
Description: Los Angeles : What Books Press, [2020] | Summary: "One young
    father reconciles his parental responsibilities with hatemongers living
    down the block, another struggles with his own parents' deaths. Fabulist
    political tales offer resistance, whether in acts of civil or psychic
    disobedience." -- Provided by publisher.
Identifiers: LCCN 2020027462 | ISBN 9780984578276 (paperback)
Classification: LCC PS3620.O5834 A6 2020 | DDC 813/.6--dc23
LC record available at https://lccn.loc.gov/2020027462

Cover art: Gronk, *untitled*, 2020
Book design by Ash Good, www.ashgood.design

What Books Press
363 South Topanga Canyon Boulevard
Topanga, CA 90290

WHATBOOKSPRESS.COM

KEEPING TAHOE BLUE
AND OTHER
PROVOCATIONS

For Lisa

and in memory of Peter Carr, artist, teacher, activist.

CONTENTS

"I live in terror of not being misunderstood."

—Oscar Wilde

PART 1: TRAVELERS

THE NEIGHBORHOOD

AS WITH TODAY'S Mexican gardening crew, the arrival of lost
strangers at the front door, back door, or front yard of his canyon home forced
Mitchell Darnell to confront the failure of his stewardship of the funky old
manse he and his wife had purchased—now falling down—not to mention
the whole nutty concept of their home ownership at all: the whimsical fraud
of his name and hers on the mortgage of a house which he and Lucy, longtime
renters, and everybody else must know they could not actually afford, or
maintain. And then, every year for six years, the county tax assessor's cheerful
letter announcing, unbelievably, the further increase in the value of their place.

They arrived, these disoriented ambassadors of the service class, to the
once-impressive house and property which, if you squinted past fading paint
and under-tended garden, broken-down fence and cracked concrete, looked
like rich folks still lived there and not Mitchell, a part-time librarian at the
university, his sixth-grade teacher wife, and their young son. The parade of
workers included off-course teenage delivery people, appliance movers, small
round brown women housecleaners arriving in cars with "Merry Maids"
or "Maid 4 U" painted on their vehicles, telephone technicians with work
orders attached to a clipboard, mobile dog and cat groomers whose reception
would not reach so deep in the hills, insurance assessors with big cameras
and loose-leaf folders, plumbers and repair people clutching their beat-up

Thomas Guide, friends of Mitchell and Lucy's neighbors down the block. All complained they'd been driving around forever, betrayed by satellite technology or given bad directions, genuinely shocked, exclaiming over and over to Mitchell that their cell phones did not work. The canyon old-timers called them "flatlanders," these misguided visitors from the suburban Southern California basin below, who arrived at the wrong house and were forced to ask for help. They called out their plaintive "Hello" or "Excuse me" or knocked first on Lucy and Mitchell's downstairs door, confused about the location of the house's main entrance, or cautiously peeked through the screen door or rang the bell, gingerly.

Sometimes Mitchell or Lucy or their son, Sasha, saw the visitors first, on their unsteady approach. Eating brunch the previous weekend, for instance, the three of them had spotted the catering girl from their second-story living room table at the big picture window. She parked below the house, at the foot of their long, ridiculous stairway under the oak tree, got out of her old VW bug, looked around and couldn't see them. "Can we help you?" they hollered in unison from the railing, startling the young woman. It was much too far away for a real conversation, even only giving directions. "C'mon up," Lucy had offered. Maggie wore her nametag and the uniform of the upscale country home-style supermarket, a red and white polka-dotted Howdy Doody blouse with a ruffled skirt, but with a nose stud and tattoos creeping down from her upper arms and shoulder, and her blouse unbuttoned in a way which Mitchell could not help notice and admire.

They'd welcomed Maggie from above, listened to her long climb up the concrete steps, then poured her orange juice, and invited her to use the telephone. Lost was not Maggie's only problem and a half-hour later, after learning that she was also unhappy at work, estranged from her boyfriend (whose car she'd borrowed) and out of gas, Mitchell poured into her tank the extra gallon kept in the garage for emergencies and sent her on her way, to the lawn party down the way, where their neighbor, Bonnie, was waiting for trays of rolled-up meat and cheese sandwiches, salads, fruit platters and desserts.

There had been confused messenger service drivers and the blue airport van guy dressed in a windbreaker with the AirXpress logo and taxi drivers who'd said they never knew the canyon even existed. This afternoon, with Mitchell home alone, Lucy and Sasha running errands in town, the two young Mexican men found him, smiling their big smiles, offering their perfect, clear coffee and cream-colored skin along with what Mitchell recognized as caution, or perhaps the fear, completely reasonable, that they might encounter an angry dog or a resident with a weapon.

Like the other lost travelers, the pair had set aside their apprehension, apparently not so scared of being bitten or shot as of abandoning the search for their day's worksite, not so scared or discouraged or shy as to give up and turn around and exit the canyon.

And, yes, these unexpected if entirely predictable visits forced Mitchell to consider, if not answer, the question of how he had arrived here himself, to try to account for the luck and class privilege and the easy injustice of it, of them falling into what Lucy called their dream house. It was a question too complicated, too connected to other, bigger questions. So, out of penance or avoidance, justification or rationalization, he avoided answering and instead did what he could for these pilgrims from beyond, of commerce and transit and maintenance and celebration, day laborers and clerks with their outdated maps and useless telephones, cut flowers and Mylar balloons in the back seat, cakes and party spreads on the floor of a refrigerated van: he turned into Mr. Happy Welcome, a jolly docent and generous host.

He'd put on his big smile and belt out his loud friendly voice and assist the waylaid person, who was usually nervous or embarrassed at having to abandon, even temporarily, their own or their boss's or boyfriend's vehicle and climb those forty steps up from Camden Way, hike up the drive below the house, cautiously trespass, wait to be challenged while looking out for signs or sounds of the invisible killer pet, and then call ahead, through the garden, into private property and intimacy, now violated.

He'd ask, and they would offer a slip of paper or a print-out, as if proof that they belonged, or that their destination existed, as if there were some doubt. When Mitchell recognized the address or the neighbor's name, he quickly showed them the way. "Edwards family," he'd say. "Fake Victorian, blue, two houses down." He knew his neighbors like people did, if sometimes in embarrassing, if helpful, caricature. There was Wilson, the wigged-out Viet Nam combat vet who worked as an exterminator, no kidding. There was single-mom Sue the park ranger and her daughter Holly, and the Brazilians with the scary Doberman (was there any other kind?) tied up outside, the nice old lady at the end of the block with fancy curtains in her window and a plastic-wrapped *Wall Street Journal* always waiting on her drive. And there was the round house, a cinderblock 1960's-era architectural oddity. Behind Mitchell and Lucy was the hermit psychotherapist he knew only because the man had once come by to apologize for his drunken boyfriend, who'd taken out their back gate with his truck, but conscientiously sent a fix-it guy around to repair it.

Mitchell had stood outside on the flagstone porch with them and pointed or drawn a quick map, or invited them to use his landline, then walked each of these pilgrims back down the stone steps to the drive below. He occasionally chaperoned the visitors himself, on foot, all the way to the right address, cheerfully excusing the whole interruption on the grounds of practicality: "You'll never find it. Besides, I need the exercise."

He'd drop what he was doing, holler to Lucy that they had a Lost One, and invite his young son, standing there watching his dad be gregarious, to come along. The boy would grab his Razer scooter propped at the front door and strap on his helmet, familiar enough with the scene to have figured out how to, like Mitchell, make the moment—already exciting with new people and commotion—even more fun.

Mitchell would determine where the visitors were parked, often blocks away, and wait for them to get into their vehicle, then walk alongside or in front, slowly, Sasha rolling just yards ahead of the creeping truck or van or car behind them, a slow procession.

And though on these occasions Mitchell knew that he was performing something good and neighborly and true, he considered himself the last person with any real authority to be doing this. He would be seen as overcompensating, didn't have the credibility or right as a newbie to be a guide for the neighborhood. Yet walking in his slippers, flip-flops, sometimes barefoot, he'd turn around and nod, acknowledge the journey and reassure the driver. Instead of feeling as though he belonged here he saw a grown man beckoning ridiculously, a fairy tale pervert, Pied Piper or Hansel to a gullible service industry teenager driving a sedan with a magnetic sign on her car door, a crew of white tee-shirt and pants-clad house painters stuffed into the cab of a truck, a paunchy tradesman in a huge diesel-powered four-wheeler humming along, all of whose trust Mitchell suspected he did not deserve but might earn, as one should.

On this warm afternoon Mitchell immediately invited the two Mexican fellows in, fetching the phone for them. They stood in the foyer, grateful if still scared, suspicious, but interested. No matter how timid or embarrassed, visitors seemed always curious enough to look around somebody else's home, scan the high-ceilinged living room, and then sort of drift over for a look-see out the giant picture window at the hills above. They'd discover Camden Drive below, and understand that they'd been observed all along, been watched over, had not trespassed or been in danger, but held in the care of people who knew they were there, temporarily un-lost. And then they'd inevitably relax a bit, ask for a glass of water or sit down, or use the bathroom, but always compliment Mitchell on his place.

These ministers without portfolio, couriers of self-consciousness, agents of commerce, had seemed only moments earlier as hapless as a person might be, broken marionettes hoping not to be yanked up and out of the rustic rural diorama by some cruel overlord puppet master. Now they were safe, their physical bodies, autonomy and spirits —temporarily not their own—restored. It was a situation Mitchell recognized out of Beckett, which anybody who'd been lost in an unfamiliar neighborhood, broken down by the side of the road, missed a bus or a train, or been abandoned by a ride knew. No matter how temporary, how momentary, that sense of being irrevocably lost, abandoned, overwhelmed and obscured: it murdered any possibility of rescue and salvation, reduced rational, sound-of-mind citizens, competent and even otherwise excellent companions, workers, parents or siblings to infantile desperation, fear, and insecurity. And then, with modest assistance, reassurance, it would be over, like seasickness gone with the first step onto land.

The taller, handsomer Mexican man dialed the handheld phone and waited for somebody to pick up. His buddy looked around. Almost immediately, a neighbor answered. "Miss Paige?" asked the man in Mitchell's living room, round-faced, young. Then he smiled his big smile again, shrugged and handed Mitchell the phone, with the woman's voice emanating still from the earpiece.

"Hi, I'm your neighbor," Mitchell said, interrupting. "These fellas? Your crew? They're lost." He continued, quickly. "So, where exactly are you?"

He heard himself trying to artificially, prematurely get at the important, urgent part of their conversation, to avoid the tedious explanation and the introduction and the time-wasting niceties.

But of course he'd interrupted her flat-out and probably hurt her feelings, and implied in even asking her this question her failure of exactitude. She just had to know where she lived, this Paige, no last name on the work order print-out. His question probably suggested judgment, he realized, about her competence. If you lived here, after all, if you chose to reside in this fairly remote semi-rural remove from wide boulevards and street signs and sidewalks and malls, you were responsible for knowing directions, distances to within a tenth of a mile, landmarks, a page and a coordinate—in their case, *The Thomas Guide*, 78, D-4—or the MapQuest url and precise turns and stops.

"Wait. Who is this?" Paige asked, to which he declared, too fast, trying to get past the awkwardness, but sounding like some pushy know-it-all, "Your neighbor. It's Mitchell. On Camden, east side of Tree House Lane, four houses down? Maybe five hundred yards." He continued, too autobiographically, but modeling, he thought, how a real canyon person should be able to give directions, likely risking a rebuke of her again.

"With my wife, Lucy. She drives a green Corolla. We have a mini-van. I work at the college? My little boy is Sasha?"

The taller Mexican guy stood near him. He, at least, looked convinced. And hopeful. "I don't know you," said the woman. It sounded mean. "I don't know any of that," said this Paige person, no last name, no sense of direction, whom he could place not at all. She didn't know him, no, and he didn't know her either, thank you very much, though they were perhaps standing only yards from each other, must be living in houses on the same side of this small hillside enclave, in a neighborhood of maybe forty homes but where it was possible, yes, to still not know or recognize or perhaps imagine your neighbor.

So Mitchell described his house this time instead of himself, lamely offering that his was the dilapidated Cape Cod with the long staircase, the bathtub flowerbed with geraniums, the "No War on Iraq" lawn sign, the kid's tricycle parked, abandoned really, in the overgrown vinca and ivy. He felt embarrassed at how much of his life he was offering to this individual he didn't know, who didn't know him and likely didn't really want to, who might choose to object (with good reason) to any or all of the elements of the life of somebody like him, who might be writing him off by now as an eccentric, perhaps even a danger, a stalker or scam artist or who, it might turn out, didn't even live in the canyon at all.

But Paige, perhaps also reluctant about this intimacy between them, still wanted, needed her yard work crew and, so interrupted him right back.

"I'm on Live Oak Hill, halfway up, right across from the park," she said. "On Camden and Tree House. There's a white picket fence in front. I'm across from the little red cottage on the corner. You know?"

"Ah, yes," he said at first, relieved. They would get through this, he would help her, and, who knows, they might meet each other at last and be neighbors, even friends. But then he, Mitchell, competent and confident, knowing this neighborhood so well from strolling it and walking it with his son, and good with cardinal directions and professionally, temperamentally good with people, was confused, himself lost.

"No." He reconsidered. "Wait, where?"

The local park, where he'd gone so many times with his son, he of the long-abandoned trike, was where he'd met the rest of his neighbors, played with their toddlers on the climbing structure, run with their dogs, shot baskets. The park was a sound, reliable landmark, communally agreed-upon as such, along with the Community Center and the "surfboard house" and the volunteer fire station. And it was so not close at all to where this woman, this voice, said she was. In fact, the park was a full six blocks away from their narrow street, down at the foot of the hills, with a locking gate and benches out front, a warning about rattlesnakes and hours posted, closed at ten PM, no alcohol, please pick up after your dog.

"The park?" he asked.

"Yes," said Paige, his invisible neighbor who lived somewhere, but where?

"The little park across the street from…" she tried again, putting together her own equation, adding things up from the beginning again like, Mitchell thought, a mathematics word problem or the murder mystery board game, like Clue "My house, on Camden and Tree House, with the white iron bench and the picket fence, on the corner. Across from the little red cottage and the little park."

Mitchell started to ask Paige to please describe the park, then interrupted himself. That was stupid. Everybody knew the park, yes, but the *little park*?

"The little park?" he said, half asking, and still using the verbal shorthand which this conversation seemed to require. The tall Mexican man stood patiently near him, watching, listening, and likely wondering why this simple exchange was taking so long, why these two crazy rich white people could not find each other. The shorter one looked out the big picture window, then Mitchell noticed him considering the framed photos arranged on the retired school district-auction piano, of Sasha with his grandparents, of Lucy and Mitchell's wedding, of little Sasha holding the big rainbow trout he'd caught himself, landed himself, carried back from the creek all by himself.

Mitchell tried again. "You mean the doggy park, right?" he asked. "With the fence around it, next to the fire house? With the playground and the liquid ambers and the broken drinking fountain, where everybody takes their dogs?" He heard himself as he kept going, offering too many details again, asking questions, sounding like a man who could not be trusted, who was playing, or bluffing, who had never even been near the park, maybe only read about it or heard about it. But he knew he needed to get it right this time, to not waste her time, his time, and the two workers' time.

Meanwhile, the short Mexican seemed to suddenly notice the quilt Lucy had hung next to the upstairs bathroom door, with the Virgen de Guadalupe design. He motioned to his pal, who nodded. It made Mitchell feel somehow better. He had, at least, the Mother of God to assure them.

"With the backboard, Paige," Mitchell continued. "And the barbeques. Our park, right?" "No," said Paige.

"No?"

"Not that park," she said. "The park across the street from me. With the white bench. The little park. The other park. The park by *my* place."

And then, at last, he understood, discovering simultaneously, painfully, that difficult image he'd buried deep in his brain, of her house and her driveway, and her garden, and of the garage next to it, and of last season's campaign signs still stacked against its south wall, just behind the overgrown jade plant. *That* was her house.

He covered the phone's mouthpiece, but found he couldn't say anything. Instead, Mitchell shook his head and then rolled his eyes for the tall Mexican. His buddy, who'd moved closer, seemed to sense some resolution.

Of course! Mitchell thought. The woman meant that tiny triangular plot, not a park at all of course, only perhaps six feet by ten by twelve, an accident of homesteading, development, construction, call it what you wanted, history even. It was necessitated once, somehow, long ago, by the physical swerve in the road around the massive magnolia tree. It was a vacant lot with a bench on it or, if you were of a mood, the charming small legacy of the sloppy arrangement of parcels by turn-of-the-century white settlers, the original lot lines now irreconcilable with the modern world's electronic laser-survey cartography, a patch left to the public commons. It was too small to be contested or argued over, a lucky historical anachronism, a cheerful no-man's land, a bit of careless grace or neglect now embraced as community, as benign, as easy, careless unquantifiable generosity, mostly because it was just too small to matter. A fireplug marked one end, and somebody had bordered the triangle-shaped plot with railroad ties sunk into the ground with rebar. It was, at least, one of the few places in the canyon where no one dumped broken appliances or unwanted furniture, taped with their piece of paper, a hand-written one-word note reading, passive-aggressively, "FREE."

Mitchell couldn't stop himself. "That's a park?" he asked, sounding too harsh. "You mean the bench? That little spot with the bench? Dana and Chris put it there. Before they got divorced." He paused, trying to get past the image of those awful lawn placards, unable to. "But anyway, Paige," he said, not trying anymore for reasonable or generous, but distracted, irritated and drawing out her name with luxurious sarcasm, "I know where you are. I know now. I do." But, to make absolutely sure, he started again, from the top: "You are at the little intersection at Camden and Tree Top," he said, asking and stating simultaneously. "With the little red cottage across from you, and the big house kitty-corner, and the bench. And you are in the green house with white trim and, yes, the white picket fence and night-blooming jasmine and the solar outdoor lights, right?"

"It's a park," Paige insisted. "I mean, to me it's a park."

"Sorry, sure," said Mitchell. "It's a park." At least he knew now where she was, the coordinates matching something like reality, at least to him, and maybe to her, he hoped: the trees and the fences and the addresses each at last in their places, the big yellow house's crazy yapping Chihuahua out in front surviving his daily death-match of chicken played with passing cars, the mail box shaped like a barn, also painted yellow, the bronze birdbath and the old tree stump with the plastic stick-on eyes, nose and mouth like the angry apple tree faces in *The Wizard of Oz* and, yes, the racist signs. The racist signs! He and Sasha had walked by them for months now, the "Patriots Defend America!" placards with their stylized flag and rifle-bearing cartoon Revolutionary War militia figure posed next to the obnoxious candidate's too-familiar name.

Mitchell had in fact never seen this house's occupants, perhaps a good thing. They'd never been home, and he'd only speculated about the residents of the place, a rental he now surmised, who'd stacked a few dozen of the signs, full-color plastic on coat hanger wire. Leftovers, probably, from the June election. Meant for distribution to supporters of the Minuteman founder who'd actually nearly beaten the local Congressman in the primaries, extras removed from campaign headquarters after somebody had been discouraged by the reluctance of even the worst of the xenophobes and nativists in this most conservative of Republican areas to stick one of the hateful placards in their own lawn or hang in their window.

Maybe the signs had been taken home by his neighbor because she hadn't known how to otherwise dispose of this mass-produced variety of hate speech-on-a-stick. What else? Leave them in a dumpster? Recycle them? Wait for the next election, and repurpose for the new, improved appeal to hatred, self-hatred? Perhaps his neighbor had worked as a Minuteman Militia county coordinator and brought them home to store but never found time to actually put them in the garage, had taken them out of her trunk and just propped them there next to where he—or now, she, Paige was her name, yes—parked her car, a bright metallic red and white-striped Mini Cooper, which Mitchell couldn't somehow imagine a right-wing jingoist driving; too sporty and free somehow, too swinging mod-British, too liberal? Foolish, he knew. Anybody could drive, or buy, or be anything, or anybody. Anybody could live anywhere.

"Okay, fine, Paige," he said. "I know where you are now. The place with the Minuteman signs propped up against the garage wall, by the fence. Right? That's you, right?"

"What?" Paige asked.

"The Minuteman guy. The candidate. His signs. The lawn placards?" She didn't say anything for a moment.

"Oh, right," she finally offered.

But Mitchell could not, would not leave it alone.

"The racist guy for Congress, the immigrant basher, the chief vigilante, leader of those clowns who stand outside Home Depot and harass people," he continued. "That's you, Paige? That's where you live?"

Silence again. Mitchell just held the phone and waited. He'd never in his life sounded this sadistic, mean, and yet it felt good, if also still wrong. He'd walked by that house so many times. With his little son, with his only child. He'd stood there and looked around, waiting for somebody else to show up, to see, to notice. Waited for somebody else to point them out to. Later, he'd walked by slightly faster, trying to ignore the signs, to pretend. He was glad Sasha wasn't home today, or Lucy. And glad that, he supposed, the two Mexican guys probably didn't know what was going on. Except that of course they did.

"Paige?" he asked, waiting for an answer.

"Just send them over," she said. "Thank you."

"Okay," Mitchell. "I'll send them over, Paige. These two Mexican guys. To your house, by your park."

He hung up. And then, as indeed often happened, Mitchell ended up walking the visitors back down his long, steep, ridiculous stairs, over the leaves layered lightly on the concrete steps, through the low-hanging wilderness—the larger landscape hidden, of hills and sky and the outside world, all of that obscured by oak and sycamore canopy—to their small, beat-up old pickup truck where a third man sat in the truck's cab, its bed loaded with lawn mowers, shovels, rakes, leaf blower, a bright orange plastic Igloo water cooler strapped to the rear gate. They did a careful, slow Y-turn while Mitchell stood there, signaling them to back up and stop with hand signals and the occasional "Okay."

And then Mitchell started out ahead of them, walking down the narrow street. They followed, and soon he saw her, really now just a hundred yards ahead, a woman standing in front of the green house with white trim, white picket fence, star jasmine crawling up the garage wall above —if you knew where to look for them—the idiotic campaign signs stacked between the massive jade plant and the wall, across the way from, yes, the rusty old bench.

Still a full block away but getting closer, he waved. The woman, presumably Paige herself—whoever she was, waiting for him, for the Mexican workers—did not wave back. Mitchell stopped. He had walked as far as the men needed to find their way, and as far as he himself would go, could go. And so he left them there, halfway down Camden Lane, and waved their truck forward, smiling, and then turned around and walked home, back to his own house, in his neighborhood.

ACCIDENT

THE OTHER DRIVERS, to my left and right, might as well be sitting out on the cement. Of course, the cement is too hot for that. I look down and notice the freeway. Caked, cracked white paint lines. Reflective orange tabs on the simmering cement pavement. I realize I've never really seen the freeway. Not moving, I mean. It occurs to me that the freeway is just a road.

Elevated here, but really kind of old, shabby. It occurs to me that the freeway is just a road in the air. I feel genuinely concerned that it may not be safe to be parked up here, as we are parked.

The freeway shakes, though nothing moves except the hot, dry Santa Ana wind. It is oddly quiet for a freeway.

I reach for the dashboard and turn on the Eye. I tune in every afternoon, to the Eye in the Sky, the news traffic helicopter. Suddenly the Eye actually chops directly above me. I hear the sound overhead and, simultaneously, on the news radio traffic report, pointing out what it sees below. It sees me, presumably. Imagine that. The Eye sees in all directions. Screaming over the noisy machinery, it reports that things are tied up. There is an accident working, a three-car pile-up on the southbound 5. CHP is on the scene. Traffic is slowed. Drivers on both sides stop to look. Looky-loos, reports the Eye, on both sides.

With things tied up here, I'm sure it's my father's accident just ahead, southbound, around the bend, in the fast lane. Perhaps he's being eye-balled by the traffic copter. It's rush hour, Friday afternoon. We are going nowhere fast, by which I mean slow.

And faster than I care to imagine, Dad is dying. Or is perhaps already dead, lying cold and unconscious. I turn off the Eye in the Sky and concentrate instead on an ambulance. I concentrate on hospital walls, hospital floors, on the white, sterile, acoustic walls of an emergency room, its walls perforated with tiny pinpoint holes. Finally, I concentrate on my father just being alive, being rolled around the halls on a gurney. Or lying still on a table. I imagine him comforted by strong professionals in white, whose special skill it is to endure the worst parts of what I can imagine.

I'm not alone. Mother sits next to me, on the hot vinyl seat of my hugely, luxuriously immobile '69 Dodge Dart. She sits lost and trusting in the passenger seat, quietly contemplating her frightened, widowed obsolescence. Her hands, pressed together, rest tightly in her lap. She is riding through their years together but, like the traffic, she is stuck. She mumbles unfinished comforts to herself, a familiar but incomplete medley of soft, heavy syllables. They disappear into the heat of the car. One is: "I guess I should just be thankful for our." Another: "You'll never know what we had together...all the things we had, gone in a moment."

None of this seems to mean anything, really. It barely moves the air around. Sure, Dad and I have been through a lot. We don't really get along, but lately have come to an understanding. Or maybe an overstanding. I'm not really sure what it is, what we understand exactly. And while it can't be much, or might be too much of nothing, I'm not ready to give it up. I'm not ready to bury him, especially here, on the freeway, stuck in the air five miles from the Emergency Room, and nothing to show for it. No body. No car. Nothing.

So I'm embarrassed and angry at Mother's catatonic and incomplete inventory of Father's life and death. I glance her way and believe I see her counting. She counts to herself, doing a crippled tally with her frozen white hands, trying to arrange things in the sudden and unfamiliar absence of my dad. She moves her head up and down, deliberately, pausing to think for a moment. Mom mumbles again, as if she's counting again. Her hands don't actually move. She does these things around the house in her mind. Rearranges the furniture, cleans for spring, pays bills, sorts through old photographs, vacuums behind the couch. All without my father. She marries him over and over again in 1956, and counts. Bridesmaids and ushers. Pieces of silver service and tablecloths. Linens and kitchen appliances. She looks forward to their years together, which have now suddenly, neatly, arranged themselves on the Santa Ana Freeway at the Disneyland off-ramp in lines of parked cars waiting for an accident. And she counts other invisible things.

I received a phone call at work. The secretary got me. I had a phone call from my mother. Dad was hit. Someone hit him, Mom said. I got the feeling she'd been talking through the telephone long before I picked it up. It wasn't his fault, she said. It was a truck. He's in the Emergency, in Santa Ana. I waited a moment. I waited for more. That was all of it.

I arranged to pick her up at their house, in the suburbs east of downtown L.A. She'd leave work and meet me there. It was thirty miles away. I drove confidently, if insanely to the old place, taking surface streets through downtown. East on Jefferson, south on Alameda, across town on Slauson past the Farmer John's packing plant, through Huntington Park, Commerce, crisscrossing back and forth over the old railroad line in Walnut Park and then again in Watts, driving the broken cement pavement. All this to avoid the freeway, to avoid traffic. Then Atlantic Boulevard south through the industrial area to Imperial Highway, over the dry cement L.A. River and the railroad yard, the self-storage facilities and mobile home parks, and finally to the green lawn in front of the house. Mother was just coming out the front door, walking across the driveway. She walked around the front to the car, leaned into the open window. I searched her face for some clue about Dad, but she only looked back at me.

"Wait a minute," she said, "the garage isn't locked." She walked back up the driveway. First, she unlocked and removed, then replaced the combination padlock on the white painted-over garage door latch. She turned and walked across the driveway, back to the car.

I forgot what came to me in that moment, of her locking the garage door. It was something brief and valuable, but I lost it. Or it just disappeared. It disappeared into the built-up heat lying against the car windshield. If I could just concentrate through that heat I might know something, I thought. About what she was doing locking the garage door while Dad was dying in the Emergency in Santa Ana. Watching her unlock and lock the garage door padlock with her old rusty hands reminded me of something. It was a brief, mechanical moment, like the click of the padlock, clear at once and then lost immediately in dead silence and heat.

I confess. I am more frightened than I have ever been at the thought of my parents' deaths. When they are gone, I will perhaps become ward of their possessions. I will have to sell them, or live with them, or more likely, find a storage space and allow them to sit awhile in darkness behind a locked garage door in a self-storage yard beside a cement river bed in the suburbs.

If I concentrate just enough, I imagine I might know something about this situation, which evaporates in front of me. About why, for instance, she locked the garage door. I imagine that I might know something more than just how all of this all ended, though even now I consider how to tell the story. Perhaps as I usually tell it, among friends, when it becomes The Funny Story. Its hilarity is long gone now and I feel like a jerk. I'm unwilling to portray my mother as the pathetic, clownish person she is, I mean in The Funny Story.

The Funny Story: The suspense is killing him. My father, I mean. How will my mother replace him? Once she was cleaning the kitchen, scrubbing the floor in the kitchen. Then she stood up on a chair to get at the walls and the dust, to wash the ceiling. She slipped, fell on the kitchen table, which broke. One of its corners collapsed. The screws broke through the wood and it was lucky she was not badly hurt.

My mother's principle worry? The broken table. The loss of it. The cost of replacing the broken kitchen table. And, naturally, she was afraid Dad would be angry or disappointed. Instead, he laughed, and made a sign. He drew it with markers, on the back of a cardboard box lid. He hung it on the kitchen wall: "No Standing on the Table. The Management." Everyone thought it was funny. I was only ten, but even I knew it wasn't funny. It was humiliating. It was meant to humiliate her.

She laughed, feeling relieved. She pretended.

Maybe he is like that for her. Maybe he is relief about broken furniture. I consider this now, watching her count wedding gifts, a blender, vacuum cleaner, furniture. How is it for my mother now, waiting for widowhood on the freeway?

English. My father married my mother because she did not speak it. She was surely an old-fashioned European girl. She would cook and clean for him. She would climb up on tables to scrub the walls and the ceiling. She could barely speak English. And this is how they are for each other, I think. They are all they have. I mean that they, each of them, are the possession of the other, and all that they share together. And they are the possessions among them, too. The furniture is animated, the buckling chairs and cracked tables. The loss of a piece of furniture is a loss of the other. This is love of something. It is some thing.

I know what happened, and it is not at all a funny story. I looked in the fast lane for an accident, for the pieces of Dad's car, for flare ash and crumbled blue green safety glass on the paved cement while my mother and I sat on the fast lane of the freeway. My mother talked about what she would do without him. What would she do without him and all the familiar things?

English is her second or third language, I never got the story straight. She married my dad fresh off the train from New York, fresh off the boat from Europe. Could they even talk to each other?

They met at church. My mother understood nothing, not baseball or driving or American jokes. She made him an excellent housewife, cook and mother to their children. They talked about God, argued about my father's driving, watched baseball on TV. There was more. It's a funny story. Not really. My mother calls me at work. Dad was in a car accident on the Santa Ana Freeway, she says. A truck hit him. The car was totaled. I rush over to their house, and we drive all the way to Orange County, to Santa Ana, on the freeway. It's rush hour, on Friday afternoon. On the way, my poor mom's talking like Dad's not going to make it.

She's afraid he's going to die in the Emergency Room before we even get there. I'm driving like a maniac through the Friday rush-hour traffic, but we're stuck there on the freeway. So finally, nearly an hour later, we drive into the Emergency parking lot. I drop her off, she runs toward the automatic doors. And just then, Dad walks out of the hospital on his own two feet.

He's fine. Alright, he's limping, slightly. He's a little bruised. The car? Totaled. But he has totaled three cars already. Anyway, he's not dead, that's for sure. So I look at Mom, I just look at her. She and Dad stand together on the long wheelchair ramp of the Emergency entrance.

"So," I ask, "what's going on?"

I'm cautious about asking. Dad stands there, listening. He's okay, after all.

I'm still sitting in the Dodge. I'm in the driver's seat. I'm waiting for an answer

She tells us both. Of course, Dad knows. She talked to him already on the telephone, as they wheeled him in for x-rays, which she did not tell me.

I look again at my mother, who leans against Dad. I'm angry. I'm confused at her innocent and balmy deception. I know immediately what she has done.

"What have you done?" I ask her.

I'm not waiting for a real answer. I say, calmly, "Mom, I thought he was going to die."

I ask her, "Why didn't you tell me? You talked to him," I ask, "on the phone?" I say, "He was fine, right? He was okay?""

"But," I ask, "the whole way on the freeway?" I hesitate.

She doesn't understand. I see that, but I'm still angry. I yell at the top of my lungs. I am so angry and confused that I look to my father's eyes for comfort. Of all people! Standing there, I finally almost like my dad, who has today survived both my mother and his own driving.

My brother Jay shows up in the Emergency parking lot. She's called him too. Now both of us stand there yelling at her. We yell. She cowers quietly. We do this in front of the Emergency Room like opera. My dad just stands there, being quietly alive, heroic.

We have humiliated her, but she still doesn't appear to understand. English is her second language. And it is important that this doesn't go too far. Dad is all right, after all. I am driving us all back home. And the loneliness of living with someone has been made abundantly clear to me.

On Christmas Eve, we'd assemble in the family room, by the fireplace. Dad would bore us with a reading from the Bible. We'd sing carols. In German for Grandfather. In Polish for Grandmother. And finally, finally we'd open the presents. Not five minutes later, Mom and Dad would hustle around the room, collect the discarded wrapping, the paper and the bows, white crepe paper, boxes, and throw them into a huge pile in the center of the room. Then the two of them would toss the crumpled paper into the flames of the fireplace.

The next morning the kids would wake up very early. We'd scramble back into the family room to survey our presents. And always something was missing. A small toy, a Christmas card, checks, even cash, burned up in the magnificent, tidy flames of the night before. Stupid, I think. Stupid of me to remember. Of course, this is not a satisfying answer. There is some reason, after all.

I reconsider. Maybe it is just those missing things.

My anger, like my perspective, is one-dimensional, and selfish. No, I am not really trying hard enough to understand my mother's experience. I am not trying very hard at all to figure exactly how long Mom has been preparing herself for Dad's death by automobile. I received a phone call at work. The secretary came for me. I had a call from my mother.

I should not have answered it. Now, I don't. Now, at least half of the time, I don't. It's cruel, but I experiment with the idea that it might save me some grief. Dad was hit, she said.

Someone hit him. A truck. It wasn't his fault.

Everyone knows. Dad is a notoriously bad driver. He is half blind. He is legally deaf in one ear. I admit, the truck part scared me. It was meant to. It was the most frightening part of the call.

The things in the house, the other vehicle, they are waiting for my parents when we get home. Dad's car is totaled. It will be replaced by the insurance. He will replace it himself, with another automobile, and Mom will be happy again, relieved at having Dad back, who was briefly missing.

I drive home on the freeway alone. It is late at night, or it is early in the morning. I am tired, but I notice myself driving with the exaggerated caution of someone who has just seen a bloody and tragic auto wreck. I feel my way slowly through the darkness, and the supple quiet of the Santa Monica Freeway. The fog rolls in. Despite this, or because of it, cars pass me left and right.

It's suburban, I think. Whatever that means. A simple life, of resilience and malleability. But it is, in its way, clarity. Things are not murky. They are not imprecise. You see what you've got, fog or not. I think that even if they had less, my parents' possessive devotion would be no less. No less benign. No less clear, and clearly intense. Because those things would still be all, everything, they have of each other. And they have, for the most part, kept track of things. My dad, for instance. He bought a new car, a fancy sports utility vehicle, with four-wheel drive. I have to say, frankly, I like it. It has added something new to our relationship. Soon after they purchased it, the three of us went for a spin. I drove. Dad sat in the passenger seat and pointed out the features arranged on the dashboard. Mom sat quietly in the back. I glanced her face in the rear-view mirror. I could tell she was pleased.

STORYBOARD

RANCHO LOS AMIGOS HOSPITAL is a Spanish mission-style complex in the Rio Hondo Valley twenty miles southeast of downtown Los Angeles, once a nationally known medical facility for the treatment of polio myelitis, with buildings arranged among tall palms and smooth, narrow winding roads, wide green lawns and cactus. It might have been a luxury spa in Palm Springs except for the patients parked out on the patios in their iron lungs, little mirrors mounted above them like periscopes, to give them their view of the world.

As a kid, I watched a parade of these polio and spinal cord injury patients roll by in hospital gowns, strapped down on their stomachs, pushing themselves on their shiny bright gurneys or wheeling their chairs from the famous hospital to the local grocery store and back to the rehabilitation complex where most of them lived permanently. They navigated the sidewalk with traction pins in their skulls, past a vacant lot on one side of busy Imperial Highway and Apollo Park on the other, past the Cris'n'Pitts Barbeque. A trail of stale sawdust spilled out the front door of the restaurant, that bit of phony down-home country roadhouse atmospherics carried on the soles of people's shoes, on the rims of their wheels, blown out to the gutter for a dozen yards, no doubt tracked into cars and homes and back to the shining floors of the hospital wards too. The Rancho patients bought hot roast beef sandwiches and cigarettes, candy, sodas, Playboys and liquor, all presumably unavailable at the hospital, and then ate, drank and smoked together in the park.

I was ten. I delivered the local paper to a couple of Rancho's administrative offices on my bike, dodging ambulances and deadly quiet, fast-moving electric Cushman carts. There, on my parents' living room wall, is a photo of me circa 1970: a goofy boy with big front teeth on a red no-gears bike, bulging canvas bags hung from his handlebars, fifty pounds of newspaper weight uncarefully unbalanced, so that any tight turns, stops or restarts meant I might tip and fall off. I posed for that snapshot photograph tossing *The Southeast News*, one hand on the handlebars, as much as I could pose without stopping pedaling. Mom panned the Instamatic exactly right to keep me in focus.

When I visited them recently, I saw that faded photo, and plenty of others, and some of the elementary school art I'd made, if you could call it that, including the God's eye made of yarn and tongue depressors and glue. There was a soda bottle covered in plaster, shaped and painted to look like a dog with a broken neck, and a tiny piece of tin hammered and bent into an ashtray. Neither of my parents smoked. Instead, it hung on the wall for forty years as if it were a family coat of arms, albeit the coat of arms of a very small, weird family. I'd been bitten by a German shepherd on my paper route, which might account for the plaster hound's injury, revenge on my part for the tetanus shot and the warnings about lockjaw and threats about needles in my stomach.

These odd remnants of my kid-hood survived, but the kitchen doorsill, where my height and dates had been penciled, had recently been scrubbed clean. I'd always imagined those numbers would stay there, where Mom had stood me up, back straight, rested a ruler on my head, and memorialized my progress in pencil notches for eighteen years. My mistake.

Of course, I also imagined once that there would always be only more, more, more as some necessary result of there once having been so much, even of our small middle-class life in Southern California during a period of relative prosperity. I depended on the surety of a reliable past which would deliver a present and then a future. But there is no fool like the child of an old sick fool, and my mistake in thinking that what went before was always there, waiting, good or bad, right out of Ecclesiastes, a time for everything under heaven, was another big one.

After Mom's first surgery, for instance, I drove the folks home from another appointment at UCI Medical Center and we found the old bottlebrush tree cut down by the new next-door neighbor, who only smiled at decades of arboreal stewardship gone, and explained that its sap had dripped on his Camaro. Then Dad showed me what Mom had done with Ajax and a sponge to that pencil mark chronology of her only child's development. He further confided that she'd been regularly pulling up the smiling Camaro-driving next-door neighbor's plants and collecting his newspapers the moment they hit his driveway, hours before anybody else woke up, her attempt at helpful if premature recycling.

Dad locked all the doors now, scared that my mother would wander away or do a drive-by washing or a guerilla lawn-weeding or make another newspaper undelivery on somebody's house. Or maybe he did it to keep out burglars, or the boy down the block who either stole Dad's power tools from the garage or, according to him, was given them by Mom.

The once-famous polio hospital, practically across the street, suddenly had a famous Alzheimer's clinic too. Or maybe it had been there for a while, and we'd only noticed it now that we had to, like needing aluminum foil and simultaneously noticing a procession of dirty miners with their flashlight helmets and pickaxes and discovering that, surprise, you have been living right next to a bauxite mine. Anyway, the combined paralysis clinic meets memory clinic was both too far away, and too late for Mom. Geography and time conspired against us. No matter how close, the place was out of bounds for her at this stage. She couldn't—or wouldn't—remember that she had the illness, which was the funny thing about it, and so she wouldn't go back for more tests because, well, why? When we finally filled her prescription for Aricept, the memory loss drug, she hid the bottle and, like another sad punch line, she either couldn't remember where, or refused to tell us. Even worse, the cancer was back too, big-time, and Dad couldn't, wouldn't tell her.

"You know why they call it the Century Freeway, right?" Dad asked me for the thousandth time. We were on the phone, me checking in, him cheering us both up.

I laughed. Old joke.

"Because," I asked, "it took a century to build?"

There was otherwise not so much funny and, actually, the 105 Freeway had finally turned out alright, with a sleek elevated MTA Green Line train running up and down the middle of it, stretching west from Norwalk past the Watts Towers, toward LAX and then down to the South Bay, though somehow actually missing the airport altogether. Go figure.

No, Dad was okay with the funny freeway but angry over the failure of Cal-Trans or the city—whoever was responsible—to fix the numbers on the "Welcome to Downey" sign at the intersection near the house he and Mom had lived in for fifty years, near the nifty new light rail and the freeway, the Catholic high school, the cement-lined river and the county golf course. Somewhere in the miles between the southern and eastern entrances to Downey, California, as in "Welcome to—Population—Elevation," the city appeared, to anybody who noticed, and of course Dad noticed, to have gained fifty feet and lost 3,400 residents.

"Where'd they all go?" I asked.

"Darn it," he said, "that's not funny. The one up on Florence still doesn't match the one on Paramount. Son, it's been six months." Dad said "Darn it" when he meant worse, and there was plenty of that. He took care of Mom full-time now. Until her illness he'd enjoyed a retired aerospace worker's weekday afternoons spent sorting nuts and bolts out in the garage with the all-news station or the Dodgers or Rush on the AM radio, arranging his impressive collection of ancient hardware in old plastic yogurt containers and Yuban cans. Fasteners, O-rings, washers, nuts and bolts—there was a lifetime of it. All of that unlikely if solid inventory-taking was pretty much over now, replaced with doctors' appointments, blood tests, family medical histories, and daily calls from his annoying adult son, me.

It was windy and dry today. "Santie Annies," Dad called them. He was fun to talk to on the phone, jokey, going on about the sign situation and lousy city government but still falling easily enough, despite himself, into the heroic civic boosterism of a long-time resident, a proud homeowner, a guy who'd coached his kid's city sports teams and stuck with the town even as the vacant lot where a boy my age had died became a credit union, the butcher shop was replaced by a carniceria (whatever that is, he'd complain), and the famously delayed freeway had flattened a hundred homes to create—at last!—an imperfect if inspired perimeter of public conveyance around the city, in a geometric frame of roads, boulevards, bus lines, trains and freeway. My boyhood neighborhood was now completely surrounded by safe, clean, low-cost municipal transportation, with the old folks left in the middle of it and not really wanting to go anywhere, not able, and Mom unwilling to travel even that single city block for treatment at the clinic which had sometime in the 90's changed from treating people who couldn't walk to people who couldn't remember.

There were telephones in each room of their old tract house, and near each instrument a hand-lettered sign—*Phone*—with an arrow pointing at it. Other signs were equally straightforward, instructive, helpful: *You are in the Master Bedroom. This is the Office. Enjoy the Guestroom. The Kitchen is for Cooking.* And my favorite, the cheerful *Welcome to our Dining Room, Where We Eat!* And the photographs, carefully labeled by Dad, of family and friends, the living room wall completely covered: *Louis = Your husband. Glenn = Your son. Leanne = Your mother* and *You.* There were snapshots of the postman (Mr. Nguyen), the gardeners (Jose, Alessandro), and the pastor (Pastor). It looked like a police investigation layout of a kidnapping or some tornado-struck family tree, its branches scattered, broken.

A typed daily bulletin announced the day of the week and date, meal times, appointments, offered a newspaper or magazine clipping, a riddle or a joke or a "brain teaser" (God help us) or some recognizable (or not, as it turned out) item from the encyclopedia of general knowledge and everyday life, this therapeutic protocol encouraged by the counseling staff which Mom refused to see. Today Dad told me he'd reproduced the Gettysburg Address, the Twenty-third Psalm, and an article on the late Republican so-called "tax reform crusader" Howard Jarvis, sort of a "Where-are-they-now?" update about which we argued, inasmuch as we could, just for old time's sake, I guess.

"Did the article mention that Prop 13 destroyed public education in California?" I asked.

Mom and Dad were, of course, good anti-tax, anti-welfare, anti-government White Christian Reaganite Republicans.

"Darn it," he said. "Do you think that matters now?"

I did, in fact, but chose to find art, or so I told myself, not politics, in this painful if heart-warming family reconciliation scene in which my acting, bad, could easily get in the way of my directing, not much better.

The lousy little indie film I'd been making began with the shape of the rectangular grid from the "Page Finder." It moved to a close-up shot of page 705, section H-7 of *The Thomas Guide*, part of a salmon and pink-colored quadrant bordered by green boulevards and blood-red freeway arteries and the cheerful blue intersecting lines of the Rio Hondo Channel and Los Angeles River. Then came an old black-and-white photo of the house taken around 1970 by a door-to-door home photographer and the yellowed newspaper clipping about that kid, Tommy, who'd died when his tunnel collapsed in the vacant field. There was a TV commercial for a car lot which advertised its location as "Where the freeways meet in Downey," a snapshot of me posing at the former North American Rockwell facility with post-orbit Apollo astronauts in their suits and, finally, bootlegged scenes from the Vietnam movie *Coming Home*, which had been filmed at Rancho.

"H-seven," I sang on the audio track. "I'm in H-seven, and my heart beats so that I can hardly speak. And I seem to find the happiness I seek," and so on, sort of sad-sack-ily. I was actually quite unhappy with the film so far, of which I was writer, producer, star, director, photographer, best boy and principal funder, by which I mean the only funder. I had gone through a dozen color photocopies of page 705 in an effort to recreate the opening title segments of *Bonanza*, the program we'd watched on Sunday nights, but it was hard to get the paper to burn the way it had on the show, slowly, from the center out to the edges, and I kept setting off the smoke alarm in my garage. As it happened, all the mothers and wives had died on the program and, not to get too auteur on anybody, I was trying for some dark foreshadowing at the same time I was illuminating or in this case, enflaming, the past. Both *Idiot's Guide to Filmmaking* and *Documentaries for Dummies*, titles I now suspect of perhaps undermining my efforts, advised starting with place and personal voice but I just kept finding the beginning of my movie, over and over and over again.

I was disappointed with my voice as narrator, not to mention my rendition of the Irving Berlin, which I'd recorded in the throes of a sinus infection which I blamed, like everybody, liked everything, on the winds, not to mention the problem of no dancing, cheek to cheek or otherwise in the movie at all.

And I wondered how many viewers would even recognize the opening titles of the show about the widower and his sons living on the Ponderosa and how many would just be confused about why I was burning a street map.

I was thinking this might end up being a silent film, an homage to home super-eights and their jumpy narrative style, blinding white flashes, grainy specters. I thought that maybe I should give up on a commentary and a sound track and any further life-threatening special audio/visual effects and just find a way to dub in the sound I remembered them making, the tick-tick-tick of the film going through the projector's gate, that persistent whirring made from the cogs slipping in and out of the perforations in the film.

"Thousands drive by that sign," Dad continued. "It's a historic and well-traveled area." It sounded like he was reading from a Chamber of Commerce brochure. But I admit it sounded pretty good.

"People eat at the world's oldest McDonald's," Dad said. "It's a National Historic site. They take in a magnificent view of the San Gabriels. They stop to see the 'Close to You' and the 'Only Just Begun.' They stroll the many fine shops and restaurants at the old Rockwell facility, now our very own Downey Landing."

I liked the "our very own" part. Dad's speech was meant to review for both of us the not-good- at-all reasons he and Mom still lived there, alone, long after they'd retired, their friends had moved away or died, Dad couldn't drive and Mom's ovaries had begun murdering her even as her brain curled up somewhere inside her head and went to sleep.

And I wondered how much strolling anybody did now, from Best Buy to Quizno's to Home Depot to a restaurant called, weirdly, the Elephant Bar. I also had my doubts about just how many people actually made the pilgrimage to those two apartment buildings owned by the Carpenters, our most notable native son and daughter, named after their biggest hit songs. I remembered being dressed in my pajamas and robe and packed into the car at Christmas, the neighbors driving the kids on our block to see those buildings draped in white lights, with Santas and elves and snowmen, Karen and Richard's gift to their hometown, but who went there now?

"I am putting Mother on," Dad said, which sounded to me like he was playing a mean joke on her. Who wasn't? He hollered her name. We both waited—me in my living room, he in his—as she wandered from somewhere in their sad three-bedroom house to pick up an extension, but then something twitched at my feet, near where the cats had played moments earlier. I looked down to see a tiny gray lizard tail doing its spastic terrestrial sidestroke across our scuffed wooden floor. "Lights, camera, action," I reminded myself, and switched the phone to speaker, grabbed my digital camera, and captured a few seconds of the grisly nature footage, the dismembered reptilian limb obligingly scooting its way from couch to front door, a good four feet, and good especially for being dead.

And with the phone still on speaker, I wrote "Western fence lizard" on one of the three-by-five cards I kept handy, because I could. I tacked it to my living room wall, where I had assembled, like the DIY movie books advised, the "storyboard" so far on a giant corkboard, crude stick-figure drawings of my endless opening scenes, notes to myself, still photos, old magazine clippings, more notes, all of which anybody with eyes could see amounted, finally, to an embarrassing mirror image of Dad and Mom's own living room wall.

The cats made off with the lizard tail, no doubt to abandon it somewhere else, and I wondered how long it would take for ants to find it, and for them to create that thin dark line to dinner, and for me to have to get out the Simple Green and decimate the entire community. And what kind of put-on did Dad have in mind? Faking a heart attack just for laughs, or rearranging all the signs on Mom, ha ha? I considered the multiplicity of terrible jokes played on all of us lately, and nobody laughing: Alzheimer's and ovarian cancer, a "twofer" Dad called it. There were five telephones at their place, not counting the ones in the garage and out on the patio. All were rotary phones. They lived in a home arranged like a museum or an interpretive center, little tags, signs and labels on everything: vitamins, cupboards, tools, bottles, like Mrs. Alice in her Wonderland: Drink me. Eat me. Remember me. The inevitable questions Mother would ask, each question requiring that I start over from the beginning. No assuming anything now, not anymore.

"It's your son," I heard Dad whisper.

Mom took the phone. "How was school today, honey?" she asked. It took me a second to figure that one out, but then I remembered another photo of me on the wall, in my high school letterman's jacket. I would roll with it.

"Great, Mom," I said. "I'm going out for varsity this year."

"Isn't that fine," she said, clearly eager to be rid of me. "Your father and I are so proud." Dad jumped back in.

"About the sign situation," he said, interrupting.

"What's that?" asked Mom.

"I've got it, dear," he said.

"But it's Glenn," she said proudly, as if reassuring him. "He's my son!"

"I know. Mine too, dear," Dad said. "He's our son. But I want to update him. I've got it now."

"Well, here's your father," Mother announced, trying to regain some control, to save face. "He's going to update you now," she said, sounding pretty sarcastic for somebody with dementia, as if she were actually making fun of both of us now. That it was us who needed reminding that the fellow on the line was my father, that she knew exactly what we were pulling here, and that we two had clearly failed to read the agenda for today's meeting, helpfully posted on a wall in some room or other. She signed off with the Lincoln from the morning's bulletin board.

"Now," she declared, "we are engaged in a great civil war, testing whether that nation, or any nation, so conceived and so dedicated, can long endure."

"Well done, Mom. Be sure to hang up the phone," I reminded her, though I already heard her walking away and I knew she'd abandoned the instrument once again.

The phone extensions were a leftover from a decade of moon travel and the promise of a modern life of ease, speed and convenience, and perhaps of inter-galactic conversation in the future promised by NASA and manufactured over at the long-shuttered North American Rockwell facility, of the efficiency and prosperity of a busy household on a faraway planet or, closer, in your rumpus room, next to the billiards table. Old black dial rotaries, real beauts. Dad liked to keep them in case power went out, which it never did, but the difficulty with five phones was that somebody always forgot to hang up the one in the kitchen, or the one in the living room or the family room or the office and, because both of the folks were also hard of hearing, they failed to appreciate the recorded message ("If you'd like to make a call, please hang up and try again.") and three minutes of loud beeping from the Verizon people, and they could go for a full day seeming (in retrospect) not to be getting any phone calls at all, probably wondering why they'd been abandoned by the world, their kid, everyone.

Of course, I knew exactly what had happened and, as punishment for my faithfulness, their phone being off the hook messed with my own, so that although I imagined that we were disconnected from them, we were not, not ever. We were linked, in nothingness, silence, paralysis. My wife and I could not call out or receive calls on our phone until my old parents hung up theirs.

Three weeks later, my film was not any closer to done. Mom was living in Whittier, which is to say that she was doing the opposite of living. Whittier is basically Downey with hills and, it turns out, hospices, lots of them. You go there to die. See *The Thomas Guide*, page 707, G-4. From the street, the place seemed an ordinary suburban tract house, except with a ramp in front and more parking than at a normal house. The hospice care staff was kind, professional, if weird. One guy seemed afraid of patients, like they might, well, die or, as they said, "expire." He quickly changed Mom's dressing, checked her temperature, administered medication, and then rushed from her room. A big woman nurse offered us CDs to play for Mom, who was drugged, unconscious, her hypothalamus having "given up," said the woman, as if it had tried to swim to Catalina Island and not made it. The musical choices were New Age harp, cheerful Jewish children's chorus or enthusiastic Spirituals meant, as Dad put it, perhaps not thinking of where we were, to "wake the dead." Nobody laughed, but it was still funny. Mom was Lutheran, and in our religious practice we just did not ever sing like that.

I put the harp music on, mostly because I was nervous about the silence, and assured the assembled relatives that it was not going to matter to Mom anyway, which sounded like how my father had been talking about her lately, as if she weren't there, despite the fact that he and I, her sister and her old mother were assembled around a body.

I couldn't help wonder who'd lain in the room most recently, listening (or not) to selections from the improbable juke-box of musical accompaniment, this death ("expiration," they called it) soundtrack, before I walked away for almost the very last time from her big, adjustable, hydraulic hospital bed, a tiny noiseless fan clipped to the metal frame above her damp forehead and my aunt, grandma and poor father gathered around. I had the idea that I was retracing somebody else's steps, that if the room and the patio were on closed-circuit TV, we could look at old tapes and see the same small journeys made over and over again, like on a loop, of family entering and bending over to kiss their loved one, then walking circles and figure-eights and going outside for air or a cigarette or to weep and somebody putting in a CD that nobody but an unconscious person could appreciate. Outside, on the small brick-walled cement patio were two chairs, a table, and an umbrella.

The bougainvillea on the trellis was dried-out, dead. What remained of the papery orange flowers looked like they might hurt you if they brushed against your skin. Loud local TV news came from the next room, on the other side of the painted brick wall. The big lady nurse came out to check on me. That's what she said, that she was "checking on me." I understood that she wanted me back inside, that she thought I belonged there. She was probably right.

"He's deaf. He's only visiting," she said, nodding toward the patient next door. "Really, just visiting," she said, as if I'd think her complicit in some easy, terrible lie. Maybe I'd misunderstand, thinking that "visiting" was the operating euphemism here for what I knew was going to happen to Mom; in the way that "only sleeping" worked with little kids for dead pets and grandparents but clearly didn't work at all in hospices. Because "only sleeping" was in its way disappointing here, as well as dishonest, as was "only visiting" because who only "visits" a hospice? But she was serious.

"He comes once a month," she said, "for a few days' rest. For the family. Caregivers need a break too."

I asked her if I could water the bougainvillea.

"We have staff for that," she said, as if there were liability issues and somebody would get in trouble. I tilted my head and gave her my most skeptical eyebrows.

"Okay," she said.

She brought me a pitcher. I watered the plant while she watched. It made one of us feel better. I went back inside. Then Mom died.

I drove Dad home with Mom's bag of clothes, her wedding bands, her eyeglasses, her partial, all of it stuffed in a blue plastic bag by the big nurse. We took Mills Avenue southwest, through Santa Fe Springs, where it becomes Florence, driving past those landmarks you find helpfully listed in the back of *The Thomas Guide* as if, indeed, you were actually going to visit Downey, California instead of just live there: theaters, parks, hospitals, historic points-of-interest and the famous McDonald's which is, actually, *not* on the National Register of Historic Places, so that our final trip home from hospice was turning out to be a little tour, which I noted to Dad because, apparently, that was what you said when you had already said everything that you could possibly say when somebody's wife dies and she doesn't even know it.

As we drove past the erroneous "Welcome to Downey" sign, Dad couldn't help himself. He was angry, and shaking.

"Darn it," he said, "they can send a man to the moon...," which was funny too because they had, hadn't they? We both laughed, and he added, "...the assholes," which cracked us both up, by which I mean I had to pull the car over next to that stupid sign and finally perform that variety of tremory, convulsion-time weeping which had been building up in my body for hours, days, maybe weeks while Dad, strapped into his seat belt, reached over and petted me from where he sat until I finished bawling, wiped my nose and eyes and pulled the car back into traffic.

The moon capsule had always arrived a month or so post-orbit at the NASA site on its national tour, proof to an earthbound citizenry that all of it had really happened just like we saw on television: the explosive launch, the orbit, the landing, the fiery descent, the splashdown, all with everybody's proud tax money and visible re-entry burns on the capsule and real-live astronauts there to sign autographs for the families of the employees, including Dad. Now the site was a shopping center with many fine retail establishments but all I would ever see there were the trios of handsome American space-travelers wearing their suits and holding their helmets, lined up to receive congratulations, to thank the Space Division employees and their wives and kids, to sign autographs in what now was a Best Buy parking lot. To assure us all that they also existed, that they had been up there on the moon on our behalf and then come back to, of all places, Downey, California, USA, which was, based on Dad's calculations, now missing about twelve per cent of its residents, not to mention his wife.

I discovered a Carpenters' website which listed the addresses of those two apartment buildings and displayed a recent photograph of a crowd of Richard and Karen's most devoted fans posing in front of one of the apartment buildings on the dead anorexic girl-woman singer's birthday. I put that photo in my clumsy if sincere artsy fake-home movie with the little scene featuring the red ants and one where I'd discovered that lizard a few days later, still tail-less, a "blue belly" we kids used to call them, amputated, but doing fine, thank you. They famously grow their tails back.

I included some voiceover about how in my childhood there had been a whole menagerie of tiny crippled creatures: "Little yellow moths surviving with their wings torn off. Toads tortured when kids on the block let the hose run across the driveway, beetles with no legs, pill bugs permanently closed up, red ants smeared like paste on asphalt, a nest of baby mice starving in a coffee can." That was my script. I confessed to all of it, and that's how my film finally ended, if you could call it that. Almost. It pretty much just finished itself, like Mom, me finally not having much to do with it. I just gave up, as she did and, as so many failed artists, gave in to my memories and dreams, which were especially vivid after her death.

There was, however, one more scene. I woke up the morning after the interment sick with allergies from the recurring desert winds and I assembled a dramatic re-creation of my most vivid post-dead-mother night-visions, done in a series of crude if pleasing stick-figure sketches, which I drew sitting at my kitchen table, the camera perched on a shelf behind me, and me narrating. In the film I speak quietly so as not to wake my wife. In one dream I'm on a cruise with my parents and a boatload of the elderly, being spoon-fed exotic meals until we hit an iceberg and sink. There is one where Mom is at a party in her nightgown and everyone is surprised to see her, wondering if she isn't supposed to be dead. "Am I?" she asks, in the speech bubble I drew above her. And at the end, if that's what it is, if that's where I finally decide to put it, there is a crude landscape, with the silhouette of the San Gabriel Mountains in the distance. High overhead, Speedee of the world's oldest McDonald's is lit-up in the clear, dark night sky. The midget chef wears his tall hat and white uniform and, looks out from his roost above Lakewood and Florence.

In this scene, which was not so much a scene as real life, Dad calls, and I don't even bother to turn off the camera. Our conversation is about how right now it's a good time for him to sell the house, before it becomes a terrible time to sell the house, which is a time everybody promises is coming. He's lived there forever and can't imagine moving.

"People say the bubble is going to burst," he says.

Because I am drawing while I listen to him, I feel that I am getting away with something, making good use of my time, more than just wallowing. It's possible I am also missing something. I hoped that the microphone would pick up our conversation in case this turned out later to be important. You never know. Sometimes you know. Mine was, is, that basic confusion that comes with Alzheimer's, somebody else's I mean, and though they will tell you it is not a communicable disease, clearly, it is. I don't know if that's worse than hereditary. When he hangs up I find that I am adding a sketch of one of the "Welcome to Downey" signs. I can't really draw. Still, in my film, as in life, we are surrounded by pictures and photographs, and by notes and to-do lists, also careful written instructions and duplicitous signs. At some point I know that Dad will have to say goodbye to the old place. He will wave and smile on that day I finally move him out and into a one-bedroom apartment in a retirement home, and that will be a helpful bit of footage, too, if you would like to see what a straightforward record of normal, everyday human sadness and disappointment looks like, and who wouldn't, especially just now?

There is an obvious, even clumsy place left in the movie to include "The End" or "Fin" or just to include a photograph of an actual, real sign, or perhaps a photograph of my late mother. However it finally ends, I will attempt to reproduce that flap-flap-flapping sound, of the old home-movie reel at its desperate, loud, cruel disconnect from any and every kind of storytelling, with bright, painful white light and, simultaneously, the promise that it can be put away until the next time such sadness is diagnosed or is even perhaps required, hard to tell the symptoms from the illness, from all the rest of it.

PART 2:
MESSENGERS

MYCENAE

HE COULD NOT SEE himself anymore, could not even remember what he looked like.

Staring into the hotel room mirror, he saw his father or an uncle, a forty-year-old yellow-haired alcoholic with drooping eyelids and greasy whiskers. He'd worked as a translator of official government dispatches, routinely writing sloppy, false and misleading information which was disseminated across Western Europe, mostly regarding agricultural production, economic forecasts, military reforms, business trends. He drank. He lost his job finally, not because anyone, at home or abroad, complained or even noticed the inaccuracies in his translations, but due to tardiness and insubordination. He had, however, successfully challenged his firing, agreed to leave, and won a handsome financial settlement.

With the money, he would travel.

He arrived on the first of May with a duffel bag and a day pack, spent the holiday in a dark bar in a port city after the ferry ride. The locals had hung wreaths of wildflowers on doors and gates. They seemed irritated that bars and restaurants were open on May Day at all. He returned to his hotel room and traveled by bus the next morning to the walled town under the fortress near the famous ruins and the rocky beach.

His eyes were bloodshot at ten o'clock. He spoke eight languages, was tanned pink, and did not bother to bathe much. Drinking in tavernas and bars in his soiled shorts and t-shirt, he listened in on other people's conversations in English, Greek, Dutch, Spanish, German, French, Italian and Flemish. He interrupted them occasionally, leaning across a table or talking from his seat at the bar in their language. He couldn't help overhear. He so seldom got to actually speak their language. He vaunted his fluency in useless chit-chat, accepted their compliments modestly, and sat down uninvited, just to hear better, he said, for conversation, over the noise of the street.

They asked him to leave, politely, saying they wanted to spend time with their friends, thank you. They were occupied and did not wish to be disturbed now. No, he could not buy them a drink. The taverna owner or the waiter walked over in the middle of his conversation to ask if everything was all right, if everything was fine.

He boarded a city bus to the ruins, sat near a bearded young man, his little daughter on his lap, the wife sitting next to them. The young man had blue eyes, red hair and the little daughter the same. They were a bit scruffy, wanderers, he thought, hippie types. English, he thought, but free spirits. Eccentrics. The wife seemed sad, as if she had resigned all responsibility for the girl to her husband.

"Fah-fah-fah," sang the little girl, holding out the notes until she only croaked them in a rhythmic staccato, not singing at all, until the sound made her laugh and she ran out of breath and started again. He smiled at the man and his daughter. The man ignored him. The wife only stared straight ahead.

He took his time climbing the slippery rock stairs at the site. Sitting, resting on a rock at the very top of the old palace, he saw the man from the bus and his little daughter slowly, very slowly making their way toward him.

"Stone," said the little red-haired girl. "Stone. Stone. Stone. Stone."

The father held her hand, lifting her along a bit with each step. "Can't step on dirt," said the little girl. "Can't step or I'll die."

Then, as they passed him, the little girl slipped on a patch of earth in between the slick stone steps, pulling up quickly.

"Uh-oh," she said. She looked at her father, panicked, embarrassed. "Well, I guess it's okay. I don't have to die because I get one free. Just one, though."

"Of course it's okay," said the father, "Dirt is just a lot of little stones anyway."

Well, he thought to himself, that's what funny English people told children, wasn't it?

He followed a group of Australians to the entrance of the tomb, where they waited while a German tour listened to their guide explain in their language the stonework, cantilevered and pinioned to form a dome. The Germans listened carefully and responded appreciatively to the information.

Then the Australians' Greek guide explained the stonework, in English. She related the method and history of its ancient construction.

"The weight of the lintel," recited the guide, "is one hundred and twenty tons."

At this the Australians "oohed" and "aahed" and one man, next to whom he was standing, remarked that it was a mighty bloody huge stone indeed. Then the Aussies followed the guide inside the dark tomb and, as they passed the entrance, he noticed many of them reaching out to smooth the stone. Inside they talked further about the tremendous weight and their voices echoed and drowned out the guide. He followed too, wanting to speak with them. He had noted an important discrepancy in the two tour guides' descriptions. The German guide's description conflicted with that of the Greek in some very important elements.

Once inside the tomb, the voices of spoken Australian English and Greek and French merged so loudly that the noise hurt his head and he left the vault. He needed a drink. Besides, he realized, it could not possibly matter to either group. Each of them had a story, a compelling account of the construction of the famous tomb.

He had an hour until the city bus arrived, so he walked the kilometer or so to the little town near the site. He settled for a restaurant as there were no tavernas, no bars. It was not a town really, only a row of restaurants, a hotel and souvenir stands.

Inside, he found thirty tables full of the same people he'd seen at the tomb. In addition to the Aussies, there were locals and other foreign tour groups, all eating about the same meal, the manager and one waiter scurrying to keep up with the banquet.

There was no room at any of the small tables, each seating four and full of dishes of lamb and potatoes and salads. The manager offered him a table by himself. He found himself sitting just outside a wall of sound like the one he'd run from inside the tomb, here recreated in the restaurant. He shouted his order to the manager, who apologized but immediately brought him a cold beer.

After lunch, he caught the city bus back to town and saw the English family again, sitting up front. He considered moving closer to them, but realized that from their place in the front of the bus they didn't see him. When the bus arrived in town, he got out after them and followed. The little girl held her father's hand. The mother only walked along, bumping against the husband. They walked through the old town, to the park adjacent the public beach, down a gravel road lined with pine trees, oleander and orange trees full of rotting fruit. He kept his distance and again, the father held the little girl's hand and the mother only walked along with them beside. He saw them leave the road at a tree a few hundred meters ahead and when he got there, he saw the path down the rock cliff to the sea. It was a narrow dirt path, the cliff steep. He did not see the family behind the boulders and trees, and decided to go back. Then he thought he heard the voice of the little girl through the wind, a torn and unintelligible high-pitched sing-song and started slowly down the narrow path.

When he reached the small beach, covered in bleached rocks, he thought he'd lost them. How? On each side the cove was bordered by enormous boulders, sitting out in three or four feet of water. He took off his sandals and waded in. Before he reached the end of the rock, he heard the little girl's voice from the other side. "Both of you," she said. "Both of you."

He waded back to the beach and climbed over the far rock, peering just over the top of it to the hidden cove on the other side. The little girl stood naked on a small outcropping facing him, with the father, his back to him, up to his chest in the water, waiting to catch her when she jumped. The mother stood on the beach, hands on hips. All three of them were naked, pale, their clothing stacked on the beach next to the woman. The shared whiteness of their bodies surprised him, and he wondered for a moment if all people looked like that. The woman's body in particular seemed ghostly pale and bore only a small triangle of sunburned skin at her neck.

The little girl stood with her arms crossed, her red hair spread across her snowy shoulders. She squatted and spoke to the father in the water, but it was too far away to hear clearly.

The father looked at the mother while the little girl whispered to him. The mother, facing them but not looking, said something but this time smiled.

Then the man left the little white girl, stumbled up the beach through the shallow water and took the woman's hand. The two of them stepped gingerly on the rocks, bending their knees, their arms crooked. The man led the woman into the water up to her neck and together they reached their hands out to the little girl, creating with their arms a basket for her in the air just above the water line.

"Ready?" she called. "I'm going to count."

They nodded. She counted "one-two-three" and jumped, clumsily, her feet dragging, her knees bending too much, so that she really only fell down into her father's and her mother's arms.

The three of them laughed, and the little girl splashed with her hands. They waded back to their clothes, put them on quickly over their wet, pale skin. They shook their damp hair and turned toward the rock where he hid. He had wanted only to talk with them, not spy and not see them in all their naked whiteness. Now he felt he had betrayed them, taken advantage.

Pretending that he had only just arrived, he backed down the rock and lay down on the beach.

As they climbed over the top of it, he turned and looked up, greeted them, and saw immediately that the woman was blind. The father found his way down the rock and when it was time for his wife to back down the side of it, the father guided her down, reached up and took her heels and placed her feet in creases and indentations in the rock. He felt foolish, spying on a blind person. They ignored him, intent on the mother. Then the little girl followed.

He smiled weakly and again felt that he had, sadly, somehow betrayed them. He perceived them as vulnerable, shy animals who lived innocent lives which others, like him, were not meant to witness, and that he had seen them defenseless, exposed, like strange creatures momentarily out of their shells.

Again, the father took the daughter's hand, the woman walking along as they crossed the beach. He could see now that the man was talking, very quietly, to the woman, telling her where to step. When they reached the dirt path back up to the road, the three of them fell into single file, the father first and the mother resting her hands on his hips, the daughter behind them, like an elephant family in procession.

He watched them until they disappeared and then climbed over their rock and onto their beach. He stood where they had stood, noticing the wet rocks, the spots where their bodies had dripped seawater. He took off his own shorts, shirt, and sandals and walked carefully to the outcropping where the little girl had stood and waited for her blind mother to catch her. He stood there, staring down at the clear shallow water, the pale round rocks on the bottom, losing himself for he did not know how long. He startled himself back into focus, stood a moment longer on the outcropping, then counted "one-two-three" out loud and dove in head-first. He came up stunned, reached his hand to his head and felt something slick, then noticed blood from a deep gash on his forehead. His neck hurt and he felt dizzy. He sat down in the seawater, which came to his lips. He reached for bottom and dragged himself to the shore and collapsed there.

When he came to, it was nearly dark, and he was sitting with the little girl and the blind woman. He was naked, but covered in his own clothes. The little girl spoke first.

"You struck a rock," she said. "The water was too shallow, and you hurt yourself."

The mother stared out at nothing, but spoke to him, reassuringly and reached for his hand.

It occurred to him that she had no idea what he looked like and yet he had seen her naked and white.

"He's gone for help," she said. "You'll be just fine."

He spent the next day in bed at his hotel, where the father, the little girl and the blind wife visited him, along with the local Greek doctor who'd mended him and provided him pain killers. He was weak, bandaged, but would recover quickly and could, if he wanted to, travel again after a few days.

"You can go home now," said the little girl.

Yes. He could go home. Why? Because he had hurt himself? Because he had misjudged the depth of the Aegean and nearly been killed? He wondered what was different now, or if anything was different at all, and why the little girl wanted to send him home, where he was unwelcome, where he had been careless and criminal about civic life, gross national product, investment futures and population growth. Yet the repercussions of his lies, if there were indeed repercussions, would be a long time in developing. No one would see their impact for perhaps years, even generations. And when they were discovered, it would be, of course, too late.

The family wished him well, left his room, and went home to England.

The doctor pronounced him fit, and did not return. He got himself out of bed, sore and shaky. He had not had a drink in nearly two days. He felt fine. No, he felt weak, and his head hurt.

He showered, shaved, and boarded the city bus again to the ruins, sat in the seat where the family had sat two days earlier. He slowly climbed the endless steps up to the palace, this time carefully stepping only on the polished white stones and nearly passing out from the heat. At the top, he rested, feeling the blood pulse under the bandage on his forehead. He watched the visitors to the ancient site climb the path toward him: An old man with a cane. A group of noisy school kids. A tall, thin couple in their sixties, wearing matching bicycle shorts and touring caps. Japanese tourists. A French family wearing elegant straw hats with black hat bands.

Imagine! All of them were there to look at rocks. They would walk and crawl over the ancient stone and be told the same things and say the same things again and some of them would slip and fall. They would stand in the dark tomb and listen to the corruption of ancient history by tour guides. Then they would get back in buses and eat at the noisy restaurant and leave, finally. He was alone there, for the moment. All the visitors were now below, looking at the famous gates or standing up above, taking in the panorama.

Then a young man, resting a video camera in the crook of his arm, ran past him, down the ancient stairs. He wore shorts and a muscle t-shirt, hiking boots. He was well built and wore his hair short. The young man stopped a few meters below and turned around and pointed the camera back up, toward the palace. The man motioned and a young woman in a red polka dot summer dress appeared, blonde hair, radiant in love, completely self-possessed yet completely indulgent of her adoring husband. She slowly stepped down each stair and, from his position below, the young man followed her with the camera, recording each confident step. The beautiful young wife in the polka dots looked out toward the surrounding country, toward the olive groves and hills, and floated gracefully down the steps, till she reached her husband, who first kissed her, then leaped ahead two at a time down another thirty steps, where he waited again for her to continue walking. They did this until they disappeared from view and he was alone again. He stood up, felt dizzy. The couple had not said a word to each other. He walked back down the stairs, tired now. He took the city bus back to the hotel and slept.

He felt better the following day. He boarded the bus to the ruins again, this time greeted by the bus driver, who recognized him. He climbed the stone stairs to the top, sat and waited there all day. He watched. He listened. He followed a tour group to the famous tomb, where a Belgian guide, holding above her head a bright ribbon tied to a short stick, led a group. The lintel, she dutifully explained, weighed one hundred and twenty tons.

He waited for the Belgians to disappear into the tomb, then stood outside and listened. He did not want to go in there again. He turned and found the bus, and went back to the hotel.

The next morning he again boarded the bus, was again greeted by the driver, and again climbed the stairs, this time perhaps more easily. He had not, he observed, taken a drink in four days. Neither had he spoken to anyone. He sat on a rock all morning and then it rained. The steps up were slippery and dangerous, but still the crowds climbed. The dirt in between turned into mud, and small pools formed in the shallow spots on the path. He only sat there, getting soaked. The rain stopped, a warm wind blew, and then he heard them talking. The stones, dead and ruined, were covered in wilting red poppies, grass and tiny white daisies.

They greeted him first in his own tongue. He got down on his knees, gingerly, as his head spun and ached still. He knelt over a smooth, shiny rock and listened. He heard the voices first of his own mother and father, then of a favorite teacher, of a girl he had loved and whom, he realized, he'd treated badly—why?—because she had loved him too. He heard other voices. The voices he'd heard yesterday, and the days before. Greek, German, Spanish. All the same people, he realized. His parents, the Belgians, the Australians in the tomb, the pale couple who had rescued him, the bus driver. He heard the Australian man say, "That's a mighty bloody huge stone," and laughed to himself.

Then he heard new voices, unfamiliar, which he could not remember, could not identify. Finally, he heard people speaking languages he did not recognize at all. The hill, covered in archeology, in sheep and goat paths, in olive trees and the wind, all of it spoke to him, whispering and blabbering and chattering until it blended into the unintelligible drone he'd heard earlier, in the restaurant.

He lay down on the path, his head on the smooth rock. He slept for five minutes, until a woman, an American wearing a hat designed as a small shade umbrella, woke him. "Are you okay?" she asked. "I just wasn't sure. Do you speak English?"

"Yes, I speak English," he said, as if that were the problem. "I am fluent in many languages."

The woman seemed relieved. She'd been alarmed to see him lying there, thought he'd collapsed or had a heart attack.

"I was only listening," he told her, smiling weakly.

He explained to her that the rocks had spoken and that he had gotten down to hear, but that he was tired from his accident a few days earlier and, yes, it seemed he had fallen asleep.

She suggested that he was still perhaps a little dizzy from his fall or whatever and might need to rest more.

He thanked her and tried to agree, but was reluctant to concede the talking rocks. He adjusted the bandage on his head. He stuffed a few small stones into his pocket and walked with the American woman, who held his elbow, down the hill to the row of giant double-decker tour buses, where she sat him down on a bench, shared water from her jug and then boarded a bus headed, he knew, for the restaurant down the road. She waved to him confidently from her seat at the window, gave him the thumbs-up sign and smiled. He waved back and tried to return the gesture but could not get his thumb to move.

As the bus turned the sharp corner and disappeared, he noticed himself in the traffic mirror on the other side of the street, a wide round convex disc with red and white stripes around it. He observed himself waving, then stood up and dragged himself over and stood in front of it, the contorted mirror in front of him and the view of the ruins beyond. He saw himself, head bandaged, his body flattened and rounded, the road to his right and to his left, and the remaining tour buses in the parking lot behind him. He felt dizzy and, reaching into his pocket, touched the little rocks he'd collected. He could not seem to hold them in his fist and get his hand out of his pocket too, so he gave up and lurched back to the bus bench with his fingers wrapped around the rocks, a huge bulge in his pants' pocket. He cut his trip short and flew home, where he placed the collection of twelve or fifteen smooth, small rocks on his window sill and immediately began translating. Occasionally, his head hurt, he ran a fever, but took a few of the remaining prescription pain killers and lay down.

He woke not recognizing his apartment. He listened and typed and, after a week of it, not leaving the apartment, had enough to believe he ought to share the conversations, the transcriptions, with someone else.

He walked downstairs, shakily, and knocked on his landlady's door. It was 2:00 AM. She answered, saw his face, and pallor, his swollen forehead, and immediately called an ambulance. He collapsed, and died in the hospital two days later, alone except for the beeping machines and the staff, to whom he spoke not a word.

An acquaintance from work was put in charge of his belongings, sorting them and giving them away, of notifying his family, who lived far away and were not interested. There would be no funeral, no memorial service.

Among his possessions the colleague from work found his notes, the transcripts. The man from work read those which had been translated into his own language, ignoring the others. Examples: *If I'd known there would be this much climbing, I would have worn sturdier shoes. Do not kill the women. I am sure I have been here before. Stand there and don't move. Your father and mother would not appreciate this. I regard you as a friend. Watch your step. Where is my daughter? I expected something so very different. Where is the toilet? Where are the trees? I love you, but we are running out of money. I am thirsty. There are ships in the harbor. Film is so expensive here. Can you recite some of Homer by heart?*

And: *Stone, stone, stone, stone, stone.*

THE LADY *AND* THE TIGER

*"Would it not be better for him to die at once, and go to wait
for her in the blessed regions of semi-barbaric futurity?"*

—Frank Stockton, "The Lady or the Tiger"

SHE CLOSED THE BOOK, placed it on the table, stood for the first
time and opened the narrow door, setting off the museum's silent alarm. In
the next room, corresponding to each animal, plant, insect and fish of the
sea painstakingly, lovingly illustrated in the dusty and faded text, the woman
discovered their imperfect if recognizable replicas, taxidermy, incarnations
of familiar creatures, and apparitions in bone, patchy fur, and bare wings:
skeletal hummingbirds, mastodons missing tusks, emaciated muskrats,
toothless wolves. One of each, occasionally two, as if a nod to another story.

The sky above, painted in faded blue, had peeled, its clouds torn.
Incandescent lights burned behind a weak, broken paper sun, flickering,
with the mechanical hum of permanent air conditioning the only real
accompaniment to the plastic stick-on galaxy and the diorama world below
it. Creatures stood still, lay, hovered or leapt in mid-air, or were otherwise
caught in frozen strides. The rocks, so hollow and fierce in their falsity! She
kicked at them, because she knew now that she could, her own bare foot
putting a hole into a large one, fiberglass and resin and shabby gray paint
cracking easily.

The woman took in the display of paralyzed beasts she'd known only as
they were cataloged in the ancient text, memorized, each with the priest or
the explorer's Victorian handwritten curlicue captions grown around them as

if in vines, or perhaps, yes, chains. She closed the door behind her, brought down the latch, and stepped carefully into the first of many more weakly-lit paradises meant to correspond to what had been written long ago. She stood alone with them finally, after so long! Here, at last, with the giant cats hurling themselves against lost time, or trapped and writhing in plastic black tar, shabby stuffed vultures perched in broken branches or on acres of duplicitous sandpaper boulders in a distant cobwebbed corner of an ecosystem, harrowed too-alert tiny pocket mice, each posing in the contrived and duplicitous scene of their tangled, spindly-drawn name-traps rendered so long ago.

Where to start? Each and every humbled or hurt creature demanded her careful, quick attention. It was everything to be here finally, and only her to act, no one else. A warning light went on, bathing all in pale, sickly, weak scarlet. Sensors had been tripped, more alarms perhaps would follow, the authorities would arrive. There were consequences beyond her own liberation now, security, apprehension, and the lively, bright noise filling these once-dead worlds, which would attract attention and deliver reprimand or worse.

So she moved quickly, reaching down to a snake, and then, lo, to those others which slithered and scurried, those which also crept and crawled and swam and glided. Snip, snip. The scissors loosened kingdom, phylum, class, order, family, genus, and species. Each subject shivered back to life, then disappeared, finding their ways out, scurrying, limping, dragging but departing. Perhaps they'd been waiting for her all along. They'd certainly been waiting, had no choice so that perhaps waiting was also everything. It had certainly been for her, after all, with time to read the book, forced to memorize it and to understand, and now to give them life back.

She moved quickly, confidently, easily through eras, periods, each a terrain or topography in sad miniature. Who'd organized this all to be so easily discovered, and then so easily destroyed? The room of fragile, arid deserts: bats and rattlesnake, saguaro and coyote, all freed in an instant. Then to the next: ponds and rivers and streams, estuaries and intertidal zones. The salmon which swam and leapt in freezing snow melt, the frogs that hopped and splashed tropically. The grizzly, the brown bear. The badger at last out of his hole for good.

Each she found in their places, and where each had stood, waited for so long, and for which there was now left only a faded ghastly silhouette, a beast-shaped plywood swath, a rotting perch suddenly, mercifully empty, worn monofilament dangling from above, or a nest fallen from a branch, leaving a feather or a busted limb, the living, breathing corollary scuttling or crawling or galloping or gliding away.

Snow, and tall pines awaited. Alpine plants, buried in plastic flocking. Eagles and doves soared anew as there she also performed her uncareful if urgent work, cutting and snipping and occasionally tearing, and sometimes so hard and fast that she injured her thumb and fingers, though the sensation was gratifying.

And soon the woman was underwater, yea, even swimming those streams and rivers to free the sturgeon and catfish and frog, next to the depths of the salty oceans, easily untangling dolphin and whales and manatees, reaching to free albino mollusks and set loose light-producing fish of the deepest darkness. It had been only minutes so far, and yet look what she'd done, what power she found she had to use! Grief and joy, and all that old, rotten Latin strewn on the floor, dusty red-velvet rope lines and "Do not touch the glass" plates broken, face down, artificial trees and plants upended, territories disturbed and plaster, wire, concrete wood revealed. The penguins, oh the penguins. They slipped and slid and were gone, gone, gone, out the hatch and down the slide.

And, finally, she lingered there at the vast seashore, where tiny shorebirds slowed her, if elegantly. Flocks of pelicans and gulls and godwits, yes godwits they had been named, beaks turned up, toward all which she was there to erase, in the direction of all she had been compelled to unfetter them from, to create anew, as if waiting. She hesitated, then heard her own name called, and understood the danger. She must hurry. She found she had no fear, only confidence and joy.

The invertebrates, amphibians, even spiders and fleas and sand crabs and remoras, all that once fed upon and fled from and hid and lived and died and even disappeared in the shallow eyes of humans, in their weak and cruel and sad imaginations, on behalf of these creatures she did not pause, no, only snipped and snipped even as the police sirens, boots, men shouting, gunshots sent her further down the hall, through the world, along the beaches and forests and glaciers looking now, why not, for barn, field and pen.

Domesticated animals? Yes, even they would be her purview, chickens, ducks, cattle, rabbits, goats and mighty steeds. And we know what she must have thought, what we all must think: How many more rooms, down which hall, before she'd find the high, higher, highest orders, crawling, walking stooped, hairy, then proudly erect, if self-congratulatory, too? Each and all would be unchained by her there too, from their self-confined display meant to be freed, perhaps even loved.

But what to do when, having freed the Cro-Magnon and the Neanderthal and the bonobo and the Australopithecus, the wooly mammoth and the house cat and the faithful dog she made it outside at last, to the alley, the sidewalk, the bus stop, the boulevard, returned to find her own self under the streetlights and traffic signals which guided others of her kind, those who carried inside them, still dead, what she had taken so much of and then freed, now roaming the streets: iguana, gorilla, rat, centipede, millipede, tortoise, among homo sapiens? Imagine what she could do out there too, might do, with her sharp scissors and her near-distant past, the woman once of the book, in the book, now escaped from the book, the book long forgotten and disregarded, if it ever existed. Just so.

Imagine her, all by herself, naked, tall, and lost except, standing near to her, because this is a fable, a parable, a riddle, a strong handsome young tiger, newly freed now and angry, you bet, and hungry and then observe you, yes yourself, passing by just then at that importunate moment of (let's call it) grace, either a rescuer or conspirator or accomplice or perhaps a betrayer, wondering first how such a scene could have been imagined, constructed, desired, allowed at all, if also delighted and secretly thrilled to witness it, the free woman once caged and the free tiger seeming to be together at last, and no reason, no coercion, no need or demand to have to choose, only to want to, to desire to, to help both of them, and yourself, to choose, to save both the lady and the tiger, and the rest of us, too.

THE PRISONER

"I will put my law in their minds and write it on their hearts."

—Jeremiah 31:33

THE PRISONER, KEPT in the federal super-maximum-security facility, brought out twice daily, alone, to exercise in the yard, had not been seen publicly or even photographed for a decade or more. The large, familiar coterie of uniformed guards kept their distance from him in work shifts, wearing latex gloves and paper masks, and earplugs, too, non-communicative except to point, bark, or nod. They would not risk physical touch, eye contact, not any human contact, respecting both the requirements of observing his punishment of isolation (at risk of their own) and also its singular power. There was, all had been warned, dangerous possibility of infection, both to him and, mostly, yes, to them.

He was officially on suicide watch, indefinitely, perhaps forever, glanced at thousands of times by frightened and doubting prison staff, assessed briefly, superficially for vitality and health, then quickly put out of mind until the next hourly check, day or night. They saw, and noted in the log, that he still wore the requisite orange jumpsuit and white tee-shirt, regulation slippers, lived in his room among books and a radio, was placed in restraints from the moment he left his one-man cell until arrival at the small exercise yard, where for one hour daily he performed his yogic stretching in the sun, ran in place, did push-ups (no pull-ups so as to avoid self-destruction on a horizontal bar by way of choreographed strangulation), completed his frenzied sprints and ended with a gentle jog, often singing, laughing, orating to himself, loudly, as if to an enormous invisible crowd or congregation despite being held there and in the walled-up confines deep inside the prison, which itself responded in a weirdly affirming too-loud echo, and The Prisoner always, always absolutely keeping his shirt on as ordered (!) and then being escorted back to his cell by a mute and intentionally self-deafened guard.

Early on he'd been assured, always, if only in writing, that he was here in prison forever lost to all, unremembered, both democratically and judicially ostracized, despite the vigils outside, appeals, gatherings and being the recipient we now know of more mail than anyone ever at the facility, the unit, it was called. In fact so overwhelmed was the penitentiary's staff early in his detention that a special cargo shipping container, then a second, had been provided to store it, each note and letter and gift and book and tape kept from him but ruled by the courts illegal to destroy outright, as possible evidence. These objects suggested both contradiction and a future without it. Such is the hopeful hypocrisy of the state, its confusion about the material and the spiritual. He'd been there for so long, and would be for so much longer it was believed, so that he would—it was assumed, even anticipated, insisted upon—die here, completely forgotten, when perhaps at last his correspondence would finally be available to him, and to others.

And so the near-mythic story of the unanswered, perhaps unanswerable correspondence also contributed to rumors that he'd died long ago, been murdered, taken his life, fallen ill or perhaps drifted into depression or a coma, lost speech, been lobotomized, taken a vow of silence. Infrequent were his communiqués, real or imagined, so much redacted were the actual few missives scribbled on scraps of paper and smuggled out who-knows-how, so dangerous were considered the tiny biographical elaborations as offered occasionally by lawyers or spokespersons or human rights volunteers themselves reluctant, scared, intimidated it seemed from saying the otherwise truth that another conclusion was unavoidable: that he was doing well, vigorous, physically healthy, planning to return despite all obstacles, all of it also unbelievable.

And what exactly had been The Prisoner's crime those many years ago, that act of civil disobedience which exiled him, our no-account of his self-made Monte Cristo, a man without a country, the hermit-priest-recluse of his own weird remove, a traitor and nonperson?

I am so glad you asked.

Once upon a time it had been the fate of The Prisoner to be purposely misunderstood, misapprehended, mistaken for, and misbegotten, meaning "fate" in all its prejudice of power and, yes, fatalism. He was a lone man, yes, but one whose manifesto was soon after his arrest posted on the internet despite the prohibitions, emailed, shared on social media, anticipated and then discovered after his actions, all of it there as the road map or narrow trail to explanation, however described as inexplicable and impossible. His story was quickly added to the catalog of killer-kidnappers and weirdoes, the sicki-wiki of the dangerous and the angry, yes, Eric Rudolph, Ramzi Yousef, the Kansas City Bombers, the Unabomber, or of the desperate and confused, as the self-immolating Buddhists of Saigon and Heaven's Gate cultists in their black pajamas, purple cloth and comet worship, yet another crazy prophet with a grudge, a potential schoolyard killer at his worst, another characterless arch-character in the familiar, eccentric, rough-hewn American tradition of cherry-picking a philosophical world-view and forcing it on others, another John the Baptist in eccentric dress-up (Goth, apostle, soldier) eager to become lost in his own dark woods, and finally gone native in a dead-end subconscious, wandering and striking out, then retreating like a rodent or wounded wild animal only to reappear in an act of more targeted violence, semi- automatic weapons and his own death.

Indeed, he arrived in the public square appearing to need to make his witness, clad in the perverse garb of the comic book Old Testament prophet, sandals and robe, fake beard and fright wig, attracting a modest, even above-average sized crowd of out-of-towners visiting the Mall, busloads of civic tourists from their respective if identical suburban backwaters of democratic illiteracy, hometown government and suspicion, Tea Party clownishness, meet-our- representative handshaking, all eager to be persuaded of the legitimacy of their own representation if not of Others', after taking in the sights and morning at the Smithsonian, a visit to Honest Abe's big lap, all present and accounted for in Bermuda shorts and sartorial bunting (eagles, flags, America!) and clutching and pointing cell phone cameras. Each and every one of them had until then been ignored by the bored Parks Service rangers and the capital locals, taxi drivers, map salesmen, tour leaders waiting impatiently for the arrival of another van-full of kids visiting from Who-Knows-Where, USA or oldsters on a weekend pilgrimage to the famous rising and sinking war-wall, but with time budgeted for a visit to an Indian casino on the way home, free dinner and fifty dollars in chips and nifty tote bags, too.

The sun was out, late morning, almost noon in early summer, before the drenching heat of the humid swampy capitol, legislators and jurors and bureaucrats and lobbyists emerging soon from their offices for lunch and air and aerobically restorative distraction from vicarious governing. Movement was orderly, if sluggish, and in this way the Republic itself resembled the traffic which ran through it, pumping blood through arteries, unaware of itself yet obedient to its own self-preservation.

And so he stood, a voice not crying in this publicly-managed federal wilderness but still attracting some modest interest: a quack, a malcontent but harmless until he suddenly disrobed, shedding his sandals and crazy disciple costume. The keen, practiced collective motion-detector impulse aroused by his action caused only modest reaction in the security types in the immediate area, who took notice and saw on closer inspection that he now wore, it was revealed, a flesh- colored full-body suit underneath, instantly becoming the dangerous representation of nakedness if not actually naked, and also that he carried some kind of surgical knife, the blade small enough to be obscured by average wishful, hopefully hopeless thinking yet still just large enough to unshyly reflect—and even more than that, amplify!—the sun's ray, and to glint its bright winking eye of anticipated hurt and the suborning of hopeful violence, the assembled human imagination both challenged and titillated.

His calm declaration that he would proceed with the ceremony (or whatever it was) meant that the extraction, the procedure, the self-surgery which followed was of course captured, recaptured, shared as was all human drama now, in images on video, the new digital scripture—where two or more were gathered and where we all existed, for eternity, the entire world— for consumption and liturgical explication, sharing, YouTube-style, erasing and editing and posting, as if that meant anything, or enough.

Yet it would also later be retold, reported, repeated in actual words, in print, and indeed confirmed for at least as long as these short films were up and available that he was—to consider only the facts—a young man, handsome, healthy, of ambiguous if helpfully Everymannish demeanor and physicality and ethnicity, clean shaven, of average height, born (it was later reported) in the anonymous friendly heartland, raised by wholesome and good people, no criminal record, a scholar and high school graduate who'd played ball and had a girlfriend once.

He stood there, it was at first assumed, only to offer, after all, a show, a trick, to perform a stunt, as a unicyclist juggler magician comedian, some kind of guerilla street artist, con man and the unfamiliar yet evocative outfit notwithstanding, a wannabe prophet evangelist. Then he reached into a duffel bag, a military-issue piece of surplus death-luggage, the dark olive drab if otherwise plain honest burden of the veteran, the combat soldier, perhaps the sharpshooter, but who could know? This could not be good but it turned out that he removed only a rolled-up piece of woven material, a small carpet, embroider prayer rug, Navajo souvenir, some kind of domesticating prop, a bit of theatrical material meant to assure and to delimit the space and to disarm reality. The park guards let him be, the tourists filmed and shot, the names on the long, half-buried wall nearby waited to be recited, clock towers called out noontime, and the sun illuminated it all, as expected.

Then, easily tearing at the fabric of his bodysuit he exposed his chest, the small blade held high so as to show what he could do, threaten, tease, what he might or, as it turned out would in fact do, quickly and in a single, swift, strong gesture. He buried the knife in his chest with one hand, then reached deep into the cavity and pulled out, no, scooped out his heart, easily, and lay it there on the rug on the cement in the Mall, with the reflecting pool in the background and the Great Emancipator behind him, and gulls and geese flying overhead on their journey to the Potomac.

All the while he smiled with the sublime expression of achievement, generosity, accomplishment, joy or a kind of secret virtue normally seen in the convert, repentant, believer. Except that, there it was, unbelievably, the still-beating, bleeding, pulsing heart of a human man and written upon it clearly, in gorgeous, elaborate handwriting, the very name of God, easy to see if obviously fading fast.

Police and ambulances were called, doctors summoned. He ignored the rush of the crowd, the assistance offered by law enforcement and paramedics and Samaritans good and bad. The young man stood there, tall, strong and steady, offering his heart-shaped hole, his emptiness, refusing entreaties and attention as the medical professionals, finding suddenly that they had no patient, tried instead to save the heart, dripping and shrinking, beating and bleeding, struggling in the heat, there on the rug upon the warm pavement in the wide-open space of the vast and tree'd democratic history-park among the splendor and the ghosts and the multitude disciples living and dead of a brave if shamed land, a republic of believers and slaves and slave-masters. The crowd, which doubled, tripled, quadrupled quickly in size, watched and pointed, then applauded after looking across the diameter of their still-wide if shrinking circle and seeing, what else, each other, themselves, waving, a vision attainable right through the perfect hole in his body where the organ once owned by Jesus, God, Yahweh, Allah had pumped and beaten and held the man since his birth, through childhood, Sunday School and into his young adult years until now, finally, his body and mind, together at last, united, reunited, had rejected that heart, this longtime transplant patient's body finally summoning up its natural resistance to the long-standing infection.

Yes, he assured them loudly, calmly, he could surely live without that! He could live now, better, even thrive. And so could they, he said. More applause. A woman fainted. Children squealed. He held out the small, sharp silver blade to them, as if this particular instrument, however perfect for the job, might not be the only one available, as if any might do. Yes, he was fine—see?—so much better than before. Emancipated, lawless. No, he felt absolutely no remorse or guilt, he said, only freedom and generous engagement, fearlessness for the first time, living the life of a slave no more.

The authorities soon enough attempted to break up the assembly, the congregation, positioning themselves to protect the public, offering him to the crowd as mad, violent, dangerous. But he only reached down to pull out the rug from under the heart, soggy with his dark blood, replaced it in the duffel and attempted to leave, on his way to the reflecting pool shaking hands, accepting embraces from men, kisses from women and children, more applause and many wanting to insert their hands, elbows, arms in that space where his possessed, propertied heart had been and where now he beat only the air, found the vibrations of the world, hosted the infinite, substituted everything and nothing instead of where, moments earlier, the indentured organ had been, a truly empty and clear vision.

And so with a crowd gathered around him he went out from that place intent not on a killing spree but, indeed, on a Living Spree, and so disrupted the tired peace of the oppressed and the supervision of the state and its missionaries, this the result of doing nothing at all except stating the obvious, if doing it, gently, dramatically, standing there alone and achieving, slowly, complete transparency, vulnerability, shaking off the word, the scar, the name, the cruel weight and immediately walking with a lighter step, stepping into a freedom of risk and a new life of example, satisfaction and autonomy.

There were doubters, of course. Had it all been a trick of the light? Optical illusion? Photoshopping? The toy model transparent man of science class, the schematic of human anatomical learning made flesh, then un-fleshed? No, impossible, not with so many who'd seen and looked in and through and beyond, who'd watched him wave and then descend the long steps with a hole in him, to abandon on the cement the signed and delivered and imprisoned heart to the EMTs, revivalists eager to get it on ice, hook it up somewhere, breathe into and pray to it and fidget and electrically stimulate, as if that had anything to do with him anymore, with anybody, an artifact as unnecessary now as gills or wings or a tail.

Yet as he attempted to depart this spontaneous homemade theater of instantaneous liberation, the transplant extracted, the dying organ abandoned, he was of course tackled to the pavement, surrounded by FBI, Secret Service, Department of Treasury, police, uniformed and undercover, then, later, priests, commentators, elected officials, the industry of oblivion and overseers, all piling on there and in the next minutes, hours, days until Homeland Security and NSA took him away for good, for his own good, for ours. What a piece of good work was this man, so perfectly incomplete, and how much more so even, especially with a hole in him to look into, for, through, honestly, a transparent wholeness, and therefore free.

And so today and forever The Prisoner rots, we are assured over and over, heartless, godless, nameless, friendless, unmarked yet in fact, as some of us understand, is thriving if unheard, unseen, our un-hunger artist, fit and healthy. How? We do not know but we are told, by, yes, something of our own selves, or someone, his biography reconstructed by word of mouth, snippets and rumors and gossip and dream, an anecdote smuggled out of here, there, from his own dark solitary block of the prison, our once-young man kept far from the other prisoners, and even farther from those slaves of the faith outside its walls who walk freely, those with names still written over their own pasts and futures, branded and tagged and so possessed by invisible almighties, poor dumb dead giants, cruel spirits, old men in robes, these many the sheep of the few, their own physical bodies straining, all of them shepherded to resist the urgent reconciliation of the limber beauty and elegant fluid which dances with the heaviness inside, and yet nearly all lacking the courage and the easy instruction of the knife.

His banned nativity story is told and retold, the scene reassembled in graffiti and pictures, brief free-standing public displays nonetheless, dramas staged. Participants are quickly dispersed, the near-mythic re-creations of his moment quickly torn down by uniformed men with helmets and axes, removed by the authorities from D.C. to Beijing to Johannesburg, a congregation of beaten if unbroken hopefuls often left vulnerable to the faith-gangs and religious vigilantes and armed lay clergy and, saddest of all, their own timidity and fear, yet rising still, impossible to rub out.

Or is it, as many say, that the exiled man with the portal of light through him, in him, this heretic of physiognomy, is still imprisoned today because he has since then done even more inside his incarceration, his exile, further responding to the body's own needs for itself, for freedom, for the prerogative of not only clarity, excising and healing but of regeneration, too, and that the real reason for his capture and continued, permanent containment is, yes, that he has lately, it is whispered, begun to regrow, to recompose the tender red flesh-machine of his own self, making and remaking his heart, making up his own heart to catch up to, to at least match his own mind to it and more, and that written upon each now is his own name at last, no gods', no masters'?

FALLING

THE SIR JAMES TEMPLEMAN I knew liked nothing better than to
instruct the groundskeepers to dig another foxhole and install another atheist
into it. We had at the plantation, at the time of the "accident," one hundred
and forty-five full-time nonbelievers enrolled in the campus's subterranean
residency program: skeptics, freethinkers, atheists, agnostics, some of them
scientists and some academics, and some just sad, angry, bitter individuals
who took Sir James up on his offer of free room and board, as it were, and a
generous stipend upon completion of the program.

There had been only five vacancies this summer, though we at
TempleLand held every confidence that they'd soon be filled too. The holes
had, since the program's inception, become quite elaborate, cozy even, each
with carpeting and satellite, Wi-Fi and hot meals delivered by our on-site
service staff, island locals who live in the small fishing village at the far end
of the bay. Among the professional and academic anti-god crowd the place
had become, I was told, something of an easy prize, low-hanging fruit on the
foundation and conference and grants circuit. Most of them didn't take the
challenge at all seriously, and TempleLand's complex of palm-circled foxholes
was considered by them, cynically if you ask me, a de facto artist's colony or
even a kind of writer's retreat. It was a free tropical vacation away from the
lab, classroom or lecture hall, a respite from what must be for these cynics the

exhausting if otherwise unrewarding work of setting good people against the divine, the miraculous, the unknowable. And, after all, as Sir James liked to point out privately, nobody listened to or compensated them adequately for their atheism, humanism or rationalism, not at the rates he did anyway, not the secular foundations or the government, nobody except a sincere old man who loved and feared his Jesus.

Still, considering we had graduated only three scholars in five years of the program, it must be conceded that this was never what you'd call a particularly successful experiment.

Lacking what they called a control model, the secular critics asked, how would results be measured? Faith, answered Sir James, is not of the quotidian or the calculable.

This was a problem, of course, or would have been except that the problem of calculating the unknowable, the unseeable had as far as I could tell most always worked for us, and not against us, to our advantage as believers and to the disadvantage, it seemed, of the nonbelievers, who demanded more.

Sir James liked to speculate further that, although results of the program would be, like the divine itself, indeed difficult to prove in their terms, to quantify, these results would nonetheless exist, publicly revealed or not, documented or not. There would be, he was confident, deathbed conversions and secret confessions, children of our alumni baptized in private. There would be doubt and prayer, and submission and redemption that no one would ever, ever know about except, yes, our Lord and Savior. Hard hearts would be softened. For that possibility Sir James Templeman, philanthropist, was willing to spend a few million dollars of a fortune one hundred times that size, built on faith and, yes, on prudent investing in commercial real estate and mutual funds.

Sir James took his tea each morning in the solarium of the main residence, among his beloved prizewinning orchids, often with a guest of the foundation who was staying with us just then, a congressman, Member of Parliament, college dean or chancellor, writer, minister, rabbi, lama or mullah. We are located on a private island in the West Indies, with guest houses, a dining room, library, landing field, swimming pool, golf course and lawn bowling, a small chapel and on-site medical support, in addition to the magnificently restored colonial mansion in which Sir James, a widower, resides. I have my own comfortable apartment in the carriage house, with a view of the sea on one side and the hills from the other.

After breakfast they often tour the grounds together, Sir James and the visiting Senator or journalist or clergyman, stopping occasionally to chat briefly with a subterranean-dwelling nonbeliever-in-residence working in his or her quarters. Walking with the aid of a cane, Sir James would point out a foxhole, and sitting inside it a well-known prizewinner, esteemed scholar, PBS host, investigative journalist or somebody else unable to resist what must have seemed the jackpot of free time to conduct research, read, collect no-strings attached fellowship money—round-trip air fare from anywhere in the world included—just to show up the famous philanthropist even while, yes, humbling himself before God if also perhaps humiliating himself in the eyes of his so-called colleagues back home. So, yes, the conversations were brief, if mostly cordial.

Friends and guests of Sir James were impressed, as might anyone be. And yet compared to the other myriad programs, this one was peanuts. The Foundation funded research and endowed academic chairs and gave away hundreds of millions annually through the International Prizes for Faith in Science. Its name alone infuriated traditional scientists, and no small number got just angry enough at us to apply for the underground residencies, nicknamed "the Holies" by a famous East Coast wag.

A residency lasted forty days, the same period Christ spent in the desert wrestling with Satan. If the participants left early, they naturally forfeited the money. But when their underground tenure was done, when they stepped out of their foxhole, each received generous compensation and could take the opportunity to elaborate on the mystical or, as more likely occurred, exercise their God-given (as Sir James liked to remind them) right to brag that they still rejected the spirit, found no evidence of it, and so had cheated the foundation after enduring five weeks in a luxurious burrow.

We were proud of our successes, however few. The three men who'd indeed come to embrace the divine, to find faith, were a Danish chemist, an American MBA, and an Indian hydrologist. Each used their time in the foxhole to study scripture, search their souls, and write scientific papers which affirmed a spiritual dimension in, respectively, the areas of chemistry, the free market and the study of the movement, distribution and quality of water. The title of the hydrologist's report was, gratifyingly, "Living Waters," which delighted Sir James.

The three scholars had looked for and found evidence, scientific proof, of the hand of the divine, and were eager to share it. Their subsequent proposals to fund research in this important work were accepted by the Institute. They eventually left their home institutions and were given permanent positions at the Templeman Science Institute in Colorado Springs, Colorado, fully endowed research chairs, and they and their work is featured today on our website.

You might have heard that Sir James had plans beyond the foxholes and the universities. Yes, there are other proposals, big ideas in the works: a privately-funded manned space launch, a faith-based interplanetary satellite exploration program, an all-Christian professional baseball league. Mystery may be found and experienced everywhere, Sir James says, and the Templeman Fund helps to sponsor the search for it. I looked forward to helping him realize this dream as his secretary, his trusted confidante. But this was not to be, not after the disappearance of the atheist Dr. Simon Killacky, age forty-eight, a part-time Geology instructor, speech team faculty advisor and women's softball coach from a small community college in Orange County, California. He had been at the estate less than three days. An unattractive if gentle man, Killacky had been welcomed at the landing field on a Friday, provided a lei and a Bible, been driven in a souped-up golf cart to his assigned hole, and clocked in by noon, thus beginning his first day. I myself did not speak to him beyond reviewing the rules. I observed him sign our standard legal agreements, answered a few routine questions, and had no interactions with him on Saturday at all. He seemed tired, perhaps anxious, when I met him, which is what I later told the investigating authorities, who reconstructed events based on evidence found in his foxhole, which is to say very little evidence at all.

It seems Dr. Killacky ate his early evening meal on both Friday and Saturday nights, read portions of scripture and sections from textbooks and scientific journals (passages still marked with post-its), made some notes on a pad, sent a handful of emails, called his lawyer on his cell phone, used the small bathroom facility and then pulled the fiberglass roof over his hole and, it seems, went to sleep. Thus he passed his first two days, and gave no indication of any behavior other than we anticipated.

Indeed, on the second night, the authorities concluded, he retired at about the same time as on the previous though, of course, there were no witnesses. Individual foxholes are purposely distant from one another, to avoid distractions, perhaps fifty meters, and neither of the two other residents closest, a black lady Marxist historian from Oakland or a botanist from Winnipeg, noticed or heard anything. In retrospect, we might have installed sensors or even surveillance cameras except that, even now, these seem an intrusion and a violation, somehow, of the spirit of the wager, the contract, premise of what was, to Sir James's mind, both a scientific laboratory and hallowed ground.

On Sunday morning at 8:00 AM, the staff delivered Dr. Killacky's breakfast tray at the edge of his as-yet unopened residence. An hour later, observing the breakfast untouched, and concerned that he had not yet awakened, security was summoned and the opaque roof pulled back, only for the server and the security man to discover Dr. Killacky missing and, in his place a new hole, situated in the center of the previously constructed one, the carpet cut away, about a meter wide. This second hole, clearly much deeper, was very dark. The width of it, the circumference of this perfect circle—there is no other way to say this—was of a human torso.

All items in Killacky's accommodations remained, untouched, the laptop and Bible and his personal items, the scene suggesting to those who first arrived that the atheist had dug down a few feet for some reason and was perhaps trapped down there, or even hiding.

Alas, investigation of the hole quickly established that this was not at all the situation. Security summoned me almost immediately and, skeptical, I soon had to concede what was obvious if unbelievable: that this was a very, very deep hole, perhaps indeed bottomless, as our security chief, a local man, would insist over and over. And which would later seem to have pretty much been proven.

And, yes, certain facts could not be denied even early on: absent footprints or other evidence, it seemed Killacky had to still be down inside there, deep down inside of it, however shallow or deep this hole. Feeling foolish, if desperate, I directed the staff to secure first one ladder, then a longer ladder, then a length of stout rope. Then they tied that rope to a longer rope, weighted with a hammer of all things, the handiest object available, lowering and lowering it until we soon ran out of line, forty, fifty, one hundred meters, neither locating Killacky nor reaching bottom, and hearing and seeing not a thing.

News of Killacky's disappearance leaked before I could notify his wife or the authorities at the embassy, and soon the media arrived, the print reporters and TV people with cameras. I apologized to Sir James, who personally supervised the rescue attempt from his wheelchair, parked at the edge of the site. I'd been reluctant, I explained, to open up the compound to the public, but he understood and agreed that we should cooperate and provide the press complete access. "We have nothing to hide," he said.

The scene soon became a familiar one, day and night, quickly developing into the "Atheist Lost in a Hole" and the "Earth Swallows up Nonbeliever" stories with the twenty-four hour cable stations sending their celebrity anchors, and investigative reporters, these familiar on-camera personalities standing on the lawn wearing khakis and guayaberas, attempting to answer for their viewers the question of how this was possible and who Killacky was and, of course, where we were, and to explain the work of the Institute. They reminded viewers and listeners and readers of Sir James's remarkable biography, the life story of a Southern-born gentleman, Rhodes scholar, lifetime Presbyterian knighted by the Queen of England, who had renounced his U.S. citizenship and moved to the island for tax reasons and to promote the investigation of the universal and divine, to advance the consideration of the holy as part of a new model of scientific inquiry.

Soon we at the compound were working with the national police, the Red Cross, and had contracted an outfit to assemble heavy equipment toward facilitating Killacky's rescue, a crane—a block and tackle pulley really, but an industrial affair—generator, lights, and seismic listening devices. Ten hours went by, then nightfall. Soon it had been twenty-four hours, when arrived the second tragedy.

An overeager rescue dog put to work sniffing for Killacky's scent jumped into the hole, or fell, and soon Jo-Jo, a German shepherd from Wyoming, became the second subject of the search and rescue operation, her photograph appearing below Killacky's on the television screen and in the newspapers.

This continued for some days, as in "Missing Man in Hole," "Day 2" and "Day 3" and, "Man and Dog in World's Deepest Hole" and soon "Day Twelve," all of it of course profoundly disrupting life and study in TempleLand, not to mention the nearby village, so that we were soon forced to send the other resident scholars home. I chartered a small jet and handed them each their envelopes as they departed, a check for each, thanking them for their good faith effort and inviting them to visit again, on a later occasion.

Yes, I assured them, they would receive credit for days in their hole so far, and could pick up at a time convenient to them. Each expressed their various concerns for Killacky, some angrily, insisting that he had been kidnapped, even murdered, most likely by us, by me or by Sir John, speculating, as these scientists will, that what now appeared to be a seemingly perfect, symmetrically-bored vertical chasm, a tunnel really, must certainly have been there before Killacky had been installed in foxhole number 139.

As for Killacky, facts soon emerged painting an alternately gratifying and unflattering portrait, and pointed to motives which led to jokes about his handiness with a shovel or his need to disappear, and fast. Yet the notes and diagrams, scribblings and mathematical equations left in his hole themselves suggested that his reason for being at TempleLand went well beyond only a grant. There were calculations and a timeline, and rough sketches, all of which seemed to point to serious scholarship regarding the actual age of the planet and examining the record of a pre-scientific history which likely corresponded to that story outlined in, yes, holy texts.

But, disappointingly, it also emerged that he had needed cash to pay off a student blackmailing him after Dr. Killacky had done things to her in his office, nasty and wrong things which she'd memorialized on her cell phone's camera feature, and which she'd threatened to share with his wife and then with the world, to spin on her website, like straw into gold. In my immediate post-disappearance discussions with Sir James, we agreed that Dr. Killacky had not perhaps been the very best choice among applicants and that the staff and I might have vetted him more thoroughly. Sir James was disappointed, naturally, but he was never angry, and I value that moment even now when he took me aside one afternoon and explained that God worked in mysterious ways and that we might be witnesses to a phenomenon right here on the grounds which was well beyond the reckoning of mere man, and that Killacky himself was perhaps playing a role important to the moment, which might be a kind of revelation—about what he could only speculate, but would not—a revelation which would no doubt point further to the connectedness of spirit and science.

"And so," he promised, "ultimately, contribute to the success of our endeavors here."

Killacky's wife, Mrs. Judith Killacky of Rancho Santa Margarita, in Orange County, felt otherwise. She arrived on a special flight we chartered.

Mrs. Killacky resembled a well-known blonde movie actress who'd once been young and sexy but who now, middle-aged and fat, appeared on late-night television commercials pleading for starving and dying African children.

She'd recently filed for divorce, and had not even known her missing soon-to-be ex-husband was staying with us at TempleLand. Mrs. Killacky, "Jude" she called herself, was of little use to the authorities, had long suspected her husband's infidelity, and so was the subject of plenty of media attention. There were the couple's small children at home, four of them, and a suspiciously large life insurance policy, all of these reliably tawdry details assembled to provoke curiosity and inspire contempt, with even more attention paid, most of it speculation, to those available details of Dr. Killacky's work in the area of the geological record of the Earth and, surprisingly, the New Testament stories of the birth of Jesus of Nazareth. This was an unexpected development, at least to me, but Sir James seemed unsurprised, and was encouraged.

"The direction of Dr. Killacky's scientific work," he said, "will redeem him, and will vindicate our own."

Meanwhile, after just two weeks, the young woman student in possession of the sex video shared it with a British tabloid, which printed stills, for which she was compensated, it was widely believed, quite generously. Then she herself disappeared, on the same day the whole thing appeared on the Internet, on a porn site.

After four full weeks of searching and waiting, after sonar and radar, explained to me as something like an underground fish finder, after x-rays and after employing a psychic and bringing in medical forensics experts from around the world, after lowering a camera and losing not one, but two mini robotic units, the actual bottom of the hole had still not been found, the existence of a bottom had not even been established, and neither Killacky nor the dog had been located. Neither had any evidence at all been discovered of either, not in the hole or on the steep walls of the chasm or anywhere else. There was no shovel, no disturbed earth. There were no footprints.

Bit by bit the press corps abandoned the story and left the island. Embarrassed, frustrated, the authorities seemed to give up too, the local police and military, Interpol, F.B.I, the army of private investigators we'd hired, all of them packing up, defeated, and likely convinced that, in the absence of evidence to the contrary, TempleLand, Sir James and I, somebody on the plantation, Killacky himself, had, somehow, contrived to make him disappear, perhaps for the insurance money, or arrange a hoax.

With the departure of the media and the police, the area around the hole was cordoned off, a round-the-clock pair of guards posted, and a single klieg light left to illuminate the site at night.

We at TempleLand held a small commemorative service in the chapel where Sir James himself paid tribute to the lost man, offering generously that he believed in his own true heart that Dr. Simon Killacky might indeed have become Number Four on our roster of scholar converts, and might yet. Our Lazarus, Sir James called Killacky, someday to be revived, resurrected, and reborn.

He further lamented the cruel attacks on poor Dr. Killacky, who had been revealed not only, it seemed, as a philanderer and sexual predator, but as a poor scholar too, having done little research or writing, it turned out, in his field prior to his brief stay with us. The newspapers reported that he'd actually published only one paper, not in a juried scientific journal, and had in fact never completed his doctoral work so that he was not a Ph.D. after all. None of this mattered to us, said Sir James, or to an island, a nation, a world which cared so deeply for his journey, ongoing, or those who loved him, and certainly not to the Creator who directed the lives of us all.

The miraculous had occurred, Sir James insisted, and although we had at first not seen it, not recognized it, this marvel, not at all an "accident" he assured us, no, not in the mechanistic way of our secular world. The mystery would still teach the world somehow. God had chosen His servant Simon, as he'd chosen Saul and Simon Peter, on whose name and shoulders He had once built his own church, the rock on whom was anchored the faith of millions. That Killacky was, he pointed out, a teacher whose subject was the history of rocks, was further promise and assurance of His plan.

Geologists and seismologists, geophysicists and Earth Scientists of all stripe responded predictably to Sir James's remarks both at the service and elsewhere, and to his interview on *Sixty Minutes*, with anger, skepticism, speculation, with theories and more questions, suggesting the unlikelihood of an anomalous fissure. They pointed to what they called the "obviously sculpted" shape of the hole, its perfect, precise route straight down, the centerline of a cylindrical crevasse, the smoothness of the walls. They mocked us, and others, suggesting that maybe, yes, something or someone had reached up from the earth's center since, lacking any evidence of activity from the surface, maybe a giant or demon with a machine or device as yet unbuilt had been used to drill up to the surface with an auger, a drill. This image appeared in an editorial cartoon, as did many others, ridiculous and yet tapping into something exciting and appealing, which Sir James chose to celebrate.

Indeed, there was always an artist's rendering, a sketch or a digitally-assembled cutaway of the Earth, on television or printed along with articles in the newspapers. There was an illustration of the shaft with Killacky and Jo-Jo falling, for minutes or hours or days, and mathematical equations of velocity, how long it would take them to fall. There was the color-coded journey through the crust to the upper mantle, then the outer core and, finally, the inner core where the man and the dog would reach the impossible heat and be melted, as if to engage the problem and the premise, and the impossibility of each at the same time, always with a tiny cartoon dog and cartoon man.

There were interviews and commentaries by oil drilling experts and spelunkers, hydrologists including our own born-again prizewinner, survivors of underground and underwater falls and cave-ins. The constant printing and airing of that image, of the tiny man in free-fall and the faithful dog above him must have caused many, as it did me, to see them as eternally falling, and to understand falling as a journey and not an end, and to begin to appreciate that journey as somehow infinite despite, of course, being reminded, over and over, that science was working hard to find an ending—in their deaths.

But not Sir James, who insisted on the infinite. He offered that this was all God's plan, for He has a plan for us all. For He is not done with us here, and neither is His work complete. He is in control, He has used His servant Dr. Killacky, and He will reveal in His time the meaning and purpose of this phenomenon, this miraculous moment, this scientific experiment, this bringing together of the nations, of his disciples, to witness his power, glory, love and caring of a Creator who can do whatever pleases Him. Remember, said Sir James, that He has counted the sparrows and numbered the hairs on our heads and created this very world, seen and unseen, so that our job, our duty, is to marvel and to wait for Him to further make real a revelation.

"Dr. Killacky is with God, and with us, somewhere," offered Sir James. "As is Jo-Jo. Because God is everywhere, on the earth and inside it as well." And that place, he insisted, is forever, is infinite.

Yet soon Sir James was forced to order me to terminate the foxhole program altogether, in part on orders from the authorities, and to have the other, remaining holes filled in. I sent letters to those scholars whose research we'd been forced to interrupt, to send home, apologizing and including a second check and the requisite legal paperwork removing from TempleLand any further liability or responsibility.

The two security guards remained, even as the holes were filled in, each landscaped berm razed and squares of new grass laid in. Life as we'd known it resumed, if tentatively, and slowly, with Sir James steadfast and confident, even happy. This was the Sir James I knew, who greeted with smiles and a wave those remaining on the grounds. The disciples, we called them, those faithful hundreds who'd arrived at the site almost immediately, and who remained camped on the perimeter after the tragedy, after the departure of the media. They cooked meals on their small camp stoves and built jolly fires at night, sang and prayed and held vigil. Most seemed to have chosen to wear white, often with a skein of cloth gauze wrapped around their heads. They decorated the great lawn with crosses, candles, cans of dog food.

The earth had swallowed up a sinner, some said. He was testing a man, and mankind. Like Jonah in the belly of the whale, or Daniel in the lion's den. Some argued that a prophet, heretofore unknown, unrecognized, had been taken from us. Either way, it was a test. God had expressed His will, and would not be mocked or questioned, would only be worshipped. They were there to witness the awesome power, to be there when Dr. Killacky, God's servant, would reappear or that awesome, if immeasurable authority revealed.

It was, then, a surprise even to me, and challenged my own understanding of His power and its requirement of faith when the first disciple leapt into the hole, and the others quickly followed her. Apparently, nobody else had expected this either, stupid in retrospect, a failing, a misunderstanding for which I blame myself.

The woman who jumped did not even bother to distract the two guards, those local police officers who'd taken a break for dinner. They sat eating their suppers at sunset just a few meters from the edge of the short wall around the hole and the yellow warning tape. Eating plates of red beans and white rice, yams, roast pork, plantains, they observed her approaching from the darkness, walking into the splay of the artificial white light, thinking perhaps that she might be heading to the portable facilities we'd organized, or adding another candle to the hundreds of votive lights which flickered and waned, the smell of their wax and the heat of their flames suggesting an outdoor cathedral under the palms.

They continued eating as she approached and, as they later reported, heard only the gentlest ruffle of air in between forkfuls of dinner. They looked up and, seeing the yellow tape broken, immediately understood. A note lay on the ground, its message written in bold, elegant and clearly female handwriting on a sheet of blue-lined notebook paper: "Follow me." And the small space that had briefly been occupied—by a young woman was all they could say, veiled, slight—was left a vacuum now somehow larger than anything which surrounded it, the lawn, the palms and the night itself.

These were local men, island men, untrained, unarmed. They called out for help, and then screamed into their walkie-talkies. One ran to the main house to summon help, to alert me and Sir James, leaving the other guard alone at the hole. So that the man could offer little resistance when the rest of them approached, when the dozen other devotees who'd waited at the perimeter of the light, hiding until they'd seen the woman, Sister Alpha she'd called herself, leap into the hole, then rushed forward themselves, running together past him and then scrambling, one after the other, one onto another, and then themselves disappeared into the redemptive oblivion of faith and mystery, a place of wonder, a narrow, deep hole in the ground wherein, it was assumed, they meant to find not only evidence of their faith but perhaps, in their action, faith itself.

And so the police and the news crews returned. A handwriting expert quickly confirmed the woman's identity not as an island local but as Sarah Melissa Jean Hoolihan, age twenty, Killacky's former community college student, that young woman who'd gone missing after selling the dirty photographs and the video taken on her cell phone.

Her parents were flown out to the island, and spent some days with us, living in a guest cottage adjacent to the house in which Mrs. Killacky stayed. They were longtime practitioners of Transcendental Meditation and each morning and evening sat cross-legged near the hole for fifteen minutes, humming and being still. They otherwise cooperated with the authorities, showed little anger toward us or toward Killacky, and were concerned that their daughter, a "good girl," a "shy girl" had somehow inspired or convinced others to jump.

The Hoolihans, Sarah's mother and father, were there a week later when, once again confounded, the exploration of the hole renewed, then abandoned, the authorities accepted Sir James's proposal, and we began construction of a viewing platform, a small amphitheater surrounding the site, with a clear thick Plexiglas barrier, around the hole. Men in hardhats worked pouring cement pilings and trimming lumber, building steps and a turnstile.

It was important, Sir James insisted, that the hole itself be left open. "They might be anywhere. They might be here, with us even now."

We sat together in the rose garden, he in his wheelchair. I had been taking Paxil for a week, prescribed by Sir James's own personal physician, and yet still not sleeping well. I was not myself. My own faith in the divine, in the unknowable, in Sir James, had been shaken I don't mind telling you, and there was also the matter of a civil suit filed against us by the widow Judith Killacky and her four orphaned children, who I saw every morning at breakfast but who otherwise stayed in her quarters.

Sir James tried to comfort, to reassure me. "These children of God," he reminded me, "they also are scientists in their way. They are astronauts, explorers. Of another realm perhaps, but on an adventure we can only dream of, and envy." Sir James, aged 80, did not hesitate. His hands did not tremble. He spoke softly, but firmly. "I wish only that I could join them."

"Do you really, sir?" I asked. "Do you?"

He looked me in the face, this man of faith, his pale blue eyes searching my face. And where I had always imagined he'd found in me something deep, had encouraged it and affirmed it in me, his mouthpiece, his servant, his friend and fellow worshipper, I saw that now he looked quickly away from me. I was, I felt, no longer the receptive pool, the reflection, the loving gaze. And, not finding in me the reciprocity of understanding and faith and wisdom, the pool into which this great man-prophet might drop a pebble of that knowledge, I saw that he glanced away, out the window, and I knew then that I risked losing him.

As so I got up from the roses and I left him there in the garden and immediately walked, slowly but deliberately in the direction of whatever he might have been seeing, summoning, that element no one had proven, the dimension unseen, the realm into which I had invited myself to dwell, had been invited by Sir James, a place which for me had been as real as the plantation, the sea, the orchids in the solarium, the roses in the garden, the palms, the very stars above, and, needing to know myself whether I might be reclaimed, whether I could live there again and always, I walked across the lawn, greeted the two guards and a dozen workers in boots and hardhats, passed under the frame of the platform under construction, considered not one moment further that I would do this, removed the plastic tarpaulin which covered the hole and leapt.

I fell and fell and fell, and must also, in my falling, have fallen asleep. I had no sense of time, which was to me a relief, and I found it easy enough to hold my arms tightly at my sides so as not to limit my progress or hurt myself. I had time to think, to remember. As a child I was taken to Disneyland, not far from Professor Killacky's former home, and to a ride sponsored by the Monsanto Corporation in which visitors to the Magic Kingdom entered what appeared to be a giant microscope, ostensibly to be shrunken to microscopic size in order to visit the internal workings of the human body, the molecules and cells, or to explore the atom, the universe, I could not recall now exactly. Such, however, was my vision of myself descending, as of a grown man reduced to the size of a small one or a child, even as it seemed to me the diameter of the hole itself also narrowed, gradually.

This could have taken days, this journey, yet my vision, in direct opposite proportion to my shrinking size, only grew as I shrunk and the tunnel shrunk, broadening. And so I saw all around me a giant tableau of history, time, faith, layers and layers of geological strata corresponding, yes, directly and precisely to the story of our Creator's handiwork, the destruction, the birth, just as the missing scientist had explained in his paper, and no doubt further detailed in his notes for those who knew how to read them.

I was Jonah, and then Daniel. I was Jacob, climbing down a ladder. As I fell, I knew it was also on top of, above, and behind Dr. Killacky and the dog Jo-Jo, that I was borne on the tailwind of Sister Alpha and the twelve other disciples, even, lo, on the bodies and spirits of multitudes. I seemed not to be falling faster. My body would, I knew, reach something called free fall, a point where I would not drop any faster, but I was not sure if this was true for falling down holes, or of how gravity worked miles and miles under TempleLand and the island. I had entered the portal to another world, if not yet entered that world itself, somehow caused by looking into Sir James's wise, ancient eyes and finding nothing of myself left. I needed to be here, for him as much as for myself.

I woke after some time to darkness and coolness, reached out gingerly to touch the slick, wet walls of the tunnel, brushing them barely with my fingertips, at a speed of what felt sometimes fast, but sometimes so slow I felt I might not be falling at all. Proximity to what must have been the earth's core began to warm the tunnel, which was also a moist place. It was dark there, but not as dark as you might imagine.

And who, I wondered as I fell, is anyone to judge me, or science or Sir James? I heard his voice as I fell, and felt relief, peace, and surrender. I wondered now what everyone, except Sir James, had been so scared of. I felt more alive than I had ever been, or felt, in my life up above. Still, I expected only more, and I looked forward to reaching the end.

I heard my own voice. There was no echo here. There was no beginning after a while, not that I could recall it, not to me and not to my journey. There was no end, not to believing, not to faith, not yet anyway, and I fell, fell, fell confidently, which is a feeling unwelcome to those on the surface, frightening, but which I assure you was the anticipation and excitement of arrival. "Remember this always," was all I thought, spoke, heard, all three of them the same expression.

And when I woke, here I was in, yes, this small chamber in the very center of the planet. I had indeed become smaller, and so fit perfectly with the others, and I took my place standing in the crèche. The scene was arranged as it should have been, with Dr. Simon Killacky standing on one side, wearing a beard and robe and carrying a staff, Sister Alpha sitting in her blue gown and Jo-Jo guarding the manger.

She smiled at me, the young and beautiful Sarah Hoolihan, and then beckoned, and the humiliating scenes of her on the video and in the photographs were no more. I approached, welcoming her invitation, and peered inside the humble cradle to adore the infant and to feel, at last, the complete joy and assurance of the sight of him, here, in the world at last, that world rediscovered by a man of science and a man of faith and, lo, there he was, Sir James, a tiny baby at rest in swaddling clothes, laid in the warm, dry straw. Around us knelt and prayed the rest of the once-missing disciples wearing their purest white, with candles burning eternally around us, the grotto illuminated by the lights as well as by the bright blue eyes of the child.

And after I had adored him, and been found again in those strong and gentle eyes, I returned to my own station, where I am now, kneeling forever and eternally, together with the others here in the enduring and real world where science and hydrology will never, ever find us, and cannot deny us, no, not hidden deep in the earth's core.

MY DENIAL

"First they came for the Socialists, and I did not speak out—Because I was not a Socialist. Then they came for the Trade Unionists, and I did not speak out— Because I was not a Trade Unionist. Then they came for the Jews, and I did not speak out—Because I was not a Jew. Then they came for me—and there was no one left to speak for me."

—Martin Niemöller

FIRST CAME THE INVITATION to join the softball team hosted by the local mega-church, part of its community outreach efforts, a campaign called "Forty Days of Prayer," promoted with lawn signs throughout my neighborhood. I liked softball well enough but had of course ignored the offer, first communicated via a bulk mail circular addressed to "Resident," then made in the person of a fellow named Ron a few days later, on a Saturday morning in early fall, a roly-poly white man who knocked on my door, interrupting my work grading student research essays. Ron was a lay minister, he said, and a softball coach. He looked so much like both of these, and simultaneously, that at first, I thought I was being hoaxed, set up for one of those TV hidden-camera or public pranking shows. Still, it was a brief distraction from grading the papers, with their predictable errors in logic, rush to easy conclusions, failure to appreciate the implications of claims and lack of supporting evidence, with me reminding myself even as I read and commented that the class was not so much about remedial writing or reading or research as, finally, about thinking, responding, framing, about thinking back, as it were.

Ron stood on my porch and cheerfully suggested both that Jesus loved me—no, loved everyone!—and that I would, he felt, make an awesome and most outstanding infielder, a real contribution to the team, he said, smiling. I did not stop to wonder how he'd come to assess my catching and throwing skills sight unseen, and so very quickly, but he was a coach, after all, and I was not, or a ball player, either. I took both his oafish if humorous pandering and clumsy if unguarded proselytizing for the everyday bullshit that typifies both sports-talk and easy evangelism. Here they were, together, lucky me. Ron from VantagePoint Church™ might just as well have guessed at my likely talent at performing the Olympic hammer-throw or high-diving from the cliffs at Acapulco or, for a satisfying blend of high-risk athletics and theology, riding a camel through the eye of a needle.

I thanked him politely and sent "Coach Ron" on his way, without bothering to contradict him or mention that I did not play baseball, and that neither did I pray. There were worse things than baseball, I thought to myself, and Ron, too, though perhaps the same could not be said for prayer. I spoke none of this out loud because I felt no obligation to explain, not to him, anyway, only body-checking my own impulse. Also, I was alone, except for Ron.

Or I might have imagined speaking a wasted effort, an argument I would lose, as I would lose, I knew, with the student essays, the project of critical thinking too ambitious, finally, too constrained by all the institutional requirements, expectations, grades, the short academic quarter, the political imperative to avoid thinking, the election of a subverter of critical thought to the presidency. I thought this to myself, uselessly, playing the familiar audio file I kept on cue in my head, loud, often hitting "replay," and yet somehow returned to the stack of freshman papers, my obligation to democracy and to my profession, my devotion and my presumed passion, however waning lately. My wife and child were away, the two innocents most used to my ranting, their short visit to out-of-town friends timed to leave me free to deal with three sets of student essays, their departure a kind of sadistic gift of time apart from my family, with me alone, if completely un-alone, and presumably undistracted, but of course otherwise now completely distracted.

Within minutes of my return to the papers a beat-up late model economy car appeared at the end of our long driveway, with three passengers—two large men, one white and one black, the pair matching except in color—and a smaller, younger one, obviously in charge, thin and European looking. After peering out from the front window, the three emerged from the vehicle as if they'd been trapped in it, struggling to find their balance on solid ground. The younger man examined a slip of paper, then looked around, seeming to compare it to his surroundings, likely confirming the trio's arrival at their destination. He then made his way toward me as I emerged from the house, pausing to pick up that morning's newspaper out on the gravel drive. The other two stood at the vehicle, its doors open. The keys must have been left in the ignition because I heard the faint, incessant warning beep from the car's interior, that machine chime of alarm which never stops until the door is closed or the battery runs down, a pestering kind of unwelcome omniscience.

The young leader greeted me in what sounded like Russian, a not unwelcome pleasantry if puzzling at first. He identified himself as a missionary representing, yes, the Church of Jesus Christ of Latter Day Saints, sent to meet me specifically because, he suggested encouragingly, I was Russian. Like him, he said, calling me "Mister" and "sir," and then pronouncing my last name as if it were in fact Russian, again not unpleasingly. My name might easily be confused as such, and had been, in the past. I like Russians, at least as much as I like baseball.

Having misidentified my heritage—not that it mattered to me one way or another—we established that these dedicated proselytizers had driven all the way from Los Angeles, fifty miles, on a mission to invite me to become a Mormon, perhaps even a Russian Mormon, of all things, a potential new convert. This, the young fellow said, would allow me the opportunity to redeem not only myself but my ancestors, Russian—like his—lost to Hell or oblivion or wherever, through baptism for the dead, retroactive vicarious salvation, or some other mystical process available to adherents. I confess the details went right by me, easily, as I stood there in my yard holding the newspaper, then unwrapping it from its plastic, listening to the incessant calliope bell ringing from the automobile—an accompaniment or better— perhaps the sound of another kind of story, one that at least made sense.

Naturally, I declined the offer. No, thank you, I said. And said no more. As in the earlier episode, I kept quiet, even as I made the extra effort, however modest, of shaking my head to myself as the missionaries departed, undiscouraged, unchastened, off to find the next real or potential Russian. I waggled my head back and forth as one does, in the perhaps half-reflexive and uncontrollable, half-irresistibly purposeful public gesture (for nobody by me) of disappointment and casual contempt. If I felt anything beyond only the mild pain of time wasted, it was genuine or nearly genuine despair and pity for three men who had driven an hour—on freeways, across wide boulevards and then down a narrow county road—to save my soul and the souls of my dead real and imagined forebears, only to be made fools of by bad research or easy assumptions, misinformation somebody had given them back at soul-saving headquarters, as if the detail of my heritage, my family or genetic history, was somehow their way in to my soul, to somebody's, to anybody's.

I returned to grading, commenting. Later that morning the "Sabbath Walkers," identified by their home-made hand-painted sign, hopped and skipped by, a group of a dozen joyful and giddy Seventh-day Adventist teenagers who, black, white, brown, Asian had, it seemed, assembled at a neighbor's house for the purpose of celebrating their devotion to God in our rural community. They were out for for a beautiful hike, and, of course, to call attention to their important and joyful work.

Just moments after they passed, I heard a knock on the front door, with two Jehovah's Witnesses standing on the deck. They were dressed the part, cardboard cut-out people, the man in a cheap black suit and white dress shirt, and the woman in a modest white blouse and black skirt, stopping by, they said, to deliver me my very own copies of both *The Watchtower* and *Awake!*, journals produced, said the man, as the woman stood and smiled, to explain not just their work, but, they said, "Everything! Eternal life. How to live." We stood briefly together on my front porch, me listening—pretending to listen—while they recited their memorized appeal in their somber attire.

"No, thank you," I said, politely, without mentioning that the competition had just been by, or the study I'd heard referenced on the public radio news show just that morning, which reported that Seventh-day Adventists were, among the many Protestant cults, indeed the most racially diverse, but also the least educated and, most memorably, the most likely to reject evolution. It was the kind of detail you remembered, appreciated, offering such helpful correlation if not quite explaining everything. And only minutes earlier, for the entire world to hear. Or not. That was exactly enough information for me, I heard myself about to say to this dour pair, as if there were the possibility of a shared understanding of the absurdity of our situation, as if we three could agree on the failure of the opposing team and, perhaps expand our critique to include their own dismal work.

That insight from NPR had helpfully framed my understanding of evangelists generally, I wanted to say to them, of science-deniers, and so I felt no need to consider further their cosmology or theology. The same went for these two people wearing badges with the initials JW, as if it were the logotype of a corporation and not of a spooky faith.

Still, I accepted a copy of each magazine as handed to me by the quiet, polite woman.

The man smiled. I recognized the limits of our encounter. And I knew enough to actually understand, recognize the substitute abbreviation, the acronym, for what it was. After all, I knew something of their mission, and that their weird religion eschewed the ubiquitous Christian cross, as both idolatry and a contrarian challenge to the actual form of Christ's physical crucifixion, a misinterpretation. Imagine, I thought, the doctrinal arguments, conflicts, big theological discussion, all of it, and then ending up with a lousy badge instead of the real deal, blood, wooden, splintered—an entire sect contrived out of some fetish over how exactly He was executed.

I thanked the pair and of course did not reference my own quick internal review of comparative religion and so felt, as I closed the door, immediately awful, nearly ill from the accumulated emotional repercussions of my duplicity or cowardice, not to mention wishing that I had even more facts on JWs, not that I would ever use them, not that further insight or scholarship would make a difference.

My encounters with these religious folk and the others angered and depressed me, perhaps predictably, and not only because of the nature and purpose of their mercenary visits, their arrogance and assumptions and ignorance, their immediate false and unearned familiarity with a complete stranger. And yet as silly as perhaps it might seem to say it, I not only felt myself assaulted, abused, yes, but worse, was annoyed, no, disappointed in and ashamed of myself for not interrupting or setting them straight, for not taking them seriously or sincerely or honestly, for not—how to put it?— sticking up for myself, objecting to being reduced this way, being diminished somehow, and without resisting.

Still, I would not let them spoil the rest of my day, so far spent largely alone except, weirdly, for the believers themselves. The student essays were nearly done, after all, their predictable achievements recorded in my dismal gradebook, and so I was soon off to the farmer's market with its welcome color and crowds, adults and children strolling and shopping.

Immediately upon arriving, a pleasant old woman greeted me with a big smile and exclaimed that she remembered me, she said, from mass. This circumstance, of two believers meeting out in the secular world, seemed to make her so very happy, as if our meeting, our reunion in the public sphere were especially blessed, special, even miraculous and not the ordinary circumstance it was—as if our previous and entirely imagined communion together in the parish had some kind of resonance here, or special reverberation, or an impact on the shape of the rest of the week. "Running into you here," she said. "Imagine," she said, as if this were some unlikely or special bit of correspondence or testament to invisible if ever-present power and authority, wisdom and good. "It is so good to see you here," she said, which I could not of course help but hear as "so God to see you," no doubt exactly as she meant it.

I smiled back as she exclaimed at how "blessed" we were, and found that I could not, did not contradict her or her God-vision, and I did not explain to her that I was in fact almost always here on an early Saturday afternoon. Passersby might have assumed we were indeed old friends, fellow parishioners, or neighbors. There was conversation all around us, but nobody to address or respond to this odd if completely unremarkable-seeming circumstance to, nobody to appeal to, to corroborate. I heard only the everyday conversations of shoppers even as she assured me again that it was so very good to see me. About that I did not disagree. I was sure that she was quite happy to see me, whoever I was, whomever she imagined I might be. Why not, regardless? I was a solid person, a good husband and father and son. I was a responsible citizen and a hard-working teacher of other people's illiterate children. I followed the rules. Except now I was not so very sure I was happy at all to see myself in action, as it were, once again colluding with or lying or whatever it was I had just done—*not* done, once again—this conduct, this behavior of keeping quiet, not contradicting or objecting, retreating to silence, my difficult and obviously fake and rote and insincere (to me) politeness, reluctance, resignation—all of it, finally, both dishonest and cowardly—the action, inaction of a fraud, of a conspirator in his own silence and easy disempowerment, assuming as I did that I had some kind of power.

Instead, as I left her, I imagined what I might have said instead, basically talking to myself, a conversation, as the old joke goes, with a friend, if not a very close friend, perhaps an ex-friend. No, of course, I do not attend mass, and do not believe. That is what I should have explained to her, even argued with the old woman outright. I do not accept, I should have said, might have said but could not, did not, the obedience and slavery that is your weird allegiance to archaic and cruel religion, especially one built so elegantly on hierarchy and gangsterism, coercion and calculated lying to children, a weird death cult of delusion and ignorance, a self-regarding fairy tale of wishful thinking. I felt better, composing this undelivered speech to myself as I got myself worked up, then immediately worse as I appreciated, acutely, painfully, that I had not spoken, spoken out, or spoken back to any of them, not one of my congregation—not to the evangelical coach or the Mormons or the Sabbath Walkers or this nice old lady—and wondered why as I shopped the market's booths for fruit and vegetables, bread and fish, normally a highlight of my week, now a completely different occasion.

The old woman was old, and so an "old woman," which made it awkward because I had been raised to respect elderly people, and was committed to similarly respecting women, if for reasons perhaps condescending. Still, I told myself, however unconvincingly, that my failure, my dishonesty or cowardice was appropriate in this case because she was such a nice, warm, happy, if perhaps also demented or feeble, or lonely, deluded, diminished old lady-woman, likely harmless and therefore somehow not worth my effort, and that I was a gentle, strong, polite middle-aged man who'd been taught, trained, not to disrespect anybody, regardless of their politics or religion or station in life. And something in me, an educated and mature fellow, otherwise confident, found it wrong to risk causing pain to, of all people, an "old woman" who could in other circumstances be my own widowed grandmother, my mother or a cherished auntie, an old retired colleague, none of whom I would ever contradict or, again, risk offending despite their cheerfully insulting and anti-social behavior.

And, then, as I slung my tote bags, now full of artichokes and halibut filet, greens and seasonal stone fruit over my shoulder, there he stood, firmly in my path, blocking my exit, the Jew for Jesus, wearing his yarmulke and t-shirt with the cheerfully misappropriated Star of David and the confusing name of his chosen organization, as obviously funny, ironic or only duplicitous as, say, Lutherans for Islam or Hindus for Zoroastrianism or more darkly, Armenians for Turkey, why not? Again, there were other remarks or cruel jokes available, which I did not make and once again felt badly and ashamed, and regretted it. But still not regretful enough to turn back after passing him to offer the *truth*—such a weak and unsatisfying word just then, but still—the truth of our encounter, the reality of the scene, the actual meaning, the accurate and objective account of what was happening, what he should expect, some calling to his attention of the perverse theater he was acting out, with its oppressive and stupid rules of engagement, disrespect, and cruelty…his contempt, finally, for his own audience!

Dozens of market shoppers walked by, nobody intervening or, dare I say it, stopping to listen in or contradict or support or rescue me—or themselves!—or confront the moment, not to chastise this pest, this opportunistic and parasitic and oblivious faith-merchant.

It was turning out to be quite a weekend, religion-wise. Driving home I remembered, from my own childhood Sunday School training or a long-ago undergraduate "Bible as Literature" class the celebrated story of the Denial of Peter, as it is called, told in all four gospels, repeated from the lectern, sung in hymns and portrayed in oil painting art. A story, yes. A fabrication, a fiction of course, but that's another story. I had not thought for an adult lifetime of his shameful moments in Gethsemane, those predicted and realized three actions of repudiation by the disciple Peter, who promised his love for Jesus, who heard the rooster crow after lying three times about his association with the Son of God and who was reminded of his betrayal, his denial by a chicken. And who, after denying, realized fully his shame and wept, in repentance. I did not quite weep, but understood Peter, or tried to, my own denials mitigated by my allegiance to less dramatic expectations of everyday personal and professional life.

My wife and son returned that night, and we spent Sunday together. I finished the essays, which were no better or worse than usual, the unsatisfying but required process of assigning grades, offering comments, recording averages smoothing out and nearly disappearing any take-away or ultimate meaning, neither to the students' or my own work.

Mitigation and expectations notwithstanding, I arrived back to work on Monday to find a couple of dozen student clubs out on campus with their booths and food for sale, posters and sign-up sheets and invitations. Every religious denomination, sect, congregation, faith tradition, Bible study group, missionary project, all of them, had arranged one next to the other their completely contradictory yet ultimately complimentary messages and appeals to embrace an invisible master, to praise and commit and submit, and of course not think.

I felt mildly panicked but pleased that there would be other students, teachers, and staff there, too, a crowd of potential skeptics, a buffer of secular perception, an institutional context of protection from this otherwise uncontested expression of the irrational and of superstition. Yet as I hurried my way past the line-up toward my department, toward my office hours, I wondered if I'd somehow missed an official memo or public announcement. There should be, I thought, more people here, more citizens, other hurriers and skoffers, and students in-between classes, colleagues on their way to get coffee, the secretary I often greeted on her late-morning power-walk across campus or the maintenance fellow sweeping up leaves.

Occasionally a civic commemoration or event sneaks up on you, forgotten shift to daylight savings, urgent blood drive, the flag at half-mast—why?— or it is suddenly the World Series and you had no idea who was playing, or that Arbor Day has come and gone, explaining the new trees planted in the parking lot. Was today a national holiday, too, in addition to some under-advertised holy occasion, a day of organized confession, profession of faith, or of public recommitment, another day of prayer? Or, I wondered, had it always been like this, every day, endlessly, unremittingly, everybody assembled behind a booth with their tracts, non-believers disappeared, and me now only more especially sensitive to it after my lost weekend?

At the very end of the long row of tables and booths sat two young fellows at a card table displaying nothing at all of the accoutrements of the other outfits, no cross or star or incense or prayer rug or banner or flag, except a small hand-written sign, an expression of that variety of familiar silly undergraduate philosophical effort at calisthenics meant to impress and engage the young— often unread and simple-minded, provincial, credulous and vulnerable—and to flatter them and engage them, the *Reader's Digest* appeal, the gimmicky sales riddle, the self-important Sunday-morning huckster homily or church marquee message. "Is religion only for the poor?" read their carefully printed and mounted rhetorical question, appeal, sophomoric provocation.

They were alone, no one stopping to engage them. Where was everybody, I wondered. I slowed only slightly. "No, it's *against* the poor," I offered in a whisper, barely looking up at them. "And everybody else, too," I added, but did not stop to elaborate further, nor to argue with or confront them, or bother to wait for a response. I chuckled to myself, wickedly, childishly perhaps if happily, then continued walking, feeling simultaneously pleased if also slightly embarrassed. I had at least responded, spoken out, or mumbled out. I wished others had overheard, laughed at my joke. But what had I said, done, set in motion, if anything at all? So little, finally. I had delivered only modestly clever words, if accurate, and perhaps embarrassed two silly young dudes who might or might not have even understood my point, my polemic, and my own too-easy freshman Marxist dialectic. And so I had cheated myself, and I had cheated them of a real debate, or a serious opportunity, a conversation with an adult, probably, I speculated, the only one who had even bothered to engage—meaning insult—them.

And suddenly, and for the first time in the past two days, I felt afraid, alarmed, however irrationally, if undeniably concerned for my physical safety. Had I indeed insulted them? I hoped so. I hoped not. Might they take revenge? I almost turned around to make sure one of them had not followed me. I had certainly made a joke at their expense, if generously, I thought, with a kind of pedagogical import. Yet it was as if I had broken an easy rule, and now would learn just how profound were the consequences, what kind of punishment there might be in store for me for daring to speak out, talk back, tease, mock.

And so I walked on, briskly, only to arrive at an even larger if separate assembly, a worshipful protest or celebration, hard to tell, the men in their robes and caps, and wearing beards. They were gathered on one side and the women, covered, on the other, also in even longer robes, the women's heads and faces covered, with everyone dressed in black and performing in somber mime a choreographed ceremony of their version of ecstatic obeisance or masochistic devotion, hard to tell what exactly. Oh, how they all loved dress-up, I thought, possibly the main attraction for this variety of devotion. I walked quickly by them, this time not daring even to hear myself think, much less shake my head or offer a caustic smart-ass remark for reasons I confess I was embarrassed to confront, or only afraid. And where were other witnesses, other passersby, civic looky-loos, campus cops, or reporters from the school newspaper? Turning a corner as I made my way to my destination I was met immediately by a lone young woman with a clipboard inviting me a chance to take a "personality test" and wondering, ever so helpfully, if I had read a life-changing book. I had read many, I wanted to say. Hadn't everybody? Not this one, of course, titled *Dianetics*. "Diuretics?" I asked, quietly, nervously, half hoping she would not hear me but flirting with something of the gentle pushback or witty resistance I'd tried earlier, with the two young faux philosophers, trying to solicit a laugh or a grin, some bit of meta-cognition from her as against the horrifying sincerity she seemed to offer.

"Pardon me?" she asked.

But try as I might I found I could not summon further the will to stop to speak to her, to review the fraudulent history of her notorious cult, able only to imagine what might follow: the crazy eyes and weird enthusiasm, her desire to be transformed, to visit faraway planets and to take me, of all people, with her. There was, after all, no one else around, just the two of us there, this broad walkway, lined with trees, otherwise totally empty. She babbled on, repeating her memorized sci-fi doxology. She seemed to me both insect-like and dead, a desiccated skeleton-spirit in a living, breathing young human body. I looked around again to check, to affirm if this was again happening to me, if others saw and appreciated my encounter, perhaps a Good Samaritan arriving just then to commiserate. I calculated our distance from the worshippers, marveling—or worse, despairing—at the weird signposts on my morning's journey.

Again, nobody else seemed to be there, not to witness the moment, to laugh with me, to object, to help me find some confirmation of the unacceptable terms of this absurd encounter, to speak up and against both the young woman space-disciple and the whole premise of the circumstance itself, not to mention the nutty tenets of her pyramid scheme hustle. And maybe that is why I also did not speak out further, not even to elaborate on my winningly lame joke.

Then, because today was, it seemed, apparently the day on which I was to be tested, I walked alone another hundred feet and next came upon an assembly of disciples with their beads, crosses, incense burning, and holding blown-up posters of torn and mutilated human embryos. Life was sacred, they chanted. And, as if cooperating with them, and contradicting them, too, there stood not a dozen yards away, a huge bearded white man with a massive heavy wooden cross, its base resting in the harness hung at his shoulders and belt, its shadow cast on the walkway. He and his ugly comrade, carrying his own crudely illustrated "Repent! Sinner!" sign yelled at the top of their lungs against whores and evildoers and promising all who failed to confess their sin an eternity in flame. The presumed actual fire of his Hell was portrayed garishly on the poster, the yellow and orange and red furnace-colors of damnation leaping up at the massive black block letters of warning in a perverse infantile cartoon. Unless we knelt and sought forgiveness and redemption we would go there, he hollered, where we were promised eternal damnation, to the place of his childish rendering, the contrived nutty ecosystem of punishment, endless and deserved. I looked around, hoping others passing by would say what I was thinking as loud as I could—*Fuck you!*—but, although I imagined they were thinking it, nobody spoke it because nobody at all was passing by.

I continued to my building, hoping to get in before further interactions with the believers. As I approached its tall glass double doors, I heard sirens in the distance. And an amplified voice. And what sounded almost like gunfire. I paused, and turned to look, even as I reached for a door handle. Some hundred yards in the distance, across the large quad, emerged first one man, then another, in the beginnings of a parade of sorts, marching in camouflage gear and carrying what appeared to be machine guns—semi-automatic military weapons—each leading between them a small group of young women, girls really, their hands tied, each linked to the other, shuffling after him. Among these I immediately recognized a couple of my own students, crying and whimpering, two young women—somebody's daughters and sisters—whose beginning research essays I had just read over the weekend, leaving them comments about spelling and evidence and awkward construction of theses and appeals based on authority, and whose struggles with research and source evaluation and composition I'd understood then, mistakenly, as the worst of their problems.

And then there appeared another man, also in camo, with a machine gun, but wearing a matching balaclava, also shepherding a group of a dozen captive young women. His own group wore ropes at their wrists, as the others, barefoot, in white robes, their heads down, as if they had stepped out of the desert or mountains or jungle, or been abducted from a ceremony of some sort, captives.

Then another soldier or leader or abductor arrived, with his own group of captives, and another, in military garb but embroidered upon it the words or slogan ة واليل ا ةيلا س ملا اإلا لغربي ا ق ري فأ which, although I could not actually read them, immediately understood nonetheless, and so recognized members of the notorious Boko Haram, kidnappers of girls and young women. Here they were on the campus of a major public university in the United States, only yards from me, having apparently stepped out from the bush, from the Sambisa Forest, Borno State, northeast Nigeria, from a continent away if always, I thought from my unlikely perspective, always near, always present, always at the ready, waiting, in the mind, in the imagination and now, finally here, yes. And why not here, who knew, perhaps a local chapter or, why not a Boko student club, a Boko Haram Student Association?

I stood, in shock, speechless. What else? What next? Except that I recognized my behavior for what it was, a stupid cliché. Shocked, indeed. Not at all. And yet I was unable to resist or fight it, the arrival of my un-imagination, my expectation, my easy dread. I found no capacity, no inner resource. I had no tools, only a briefcase and a backpack. Worse, I had, it seemed, no voice. I stood, trembling, then considered that I might hide, run away, disappear, perhaps enter the faculty office building or dive into shrubbery adjacent the entrance. I looked for a colleague, student or staff person. I was alone. I looked for, searched for something in my own body with which to respond but found nothing, not in own voice or guide or secret self, nor my inner unspoken thoughts, not even my hilarious and sarcastic and pleasing whisper of subconscious. Even this, my own internal narrator-voice, failed me. I felt my politeness, timidity and accommodation, and they mocked me loudly, as did my useless and now unfunny past efforts at gentle wit or mockery. I felt physically ill. I sweated, and trembled.

I watched the men approach, with their captives. I saw what would happen now, that I would be taken, too, or that I would be shot. I felt panic and despair, but also, weirdly, relief, at the truth of my denial, however useless, now confirmed. I had indeed been weak and disingenuous, yes, but I had been right, hadn't I? I would die, here, on the steps of a university campus building, murdered if vindicated, justified if dead.

Of course, my sense of survival at last kicked in, of self-preservation, my horror at losing my dear wife and sweet child, and I dashed inside the lobby of my building, found my cell phone and called for help. The men with guns, leading the women and girls, seemed not to notice or care, and only continued walking, marching right by me, as if I were not there at all. A recording at campus security advised that I could leave a message. I hung up and ran past the elevator and up the stairs to the second floor. The receptionist was missing, the student work absent. I passed no one, other instructors' doors, usually open, now closed, the photocopy room unattended.

I unlocked and entered my own office, and looked for my office mate, who should have been there, in our messy workspace, the walls covered in posters celebrating books and movies and travel and art, with photographs of our wives and children, a fat potted cactus, a coffee maker, but otherwise every corner and surface stacked with books and notebooks, dreary journals and more, always more, student essays. I would normally have unpacked that weekend's papers from my briefcase, and settled in for a day of office hours, a staff meeting, recording grades, writing a letter of recommendation and doing administrative paperwork but from my window I saw more armed men and their prisoners. I watched, unsure if others apprehended this scene, but spotted no other witnesses, not in the windows of adjacent buildings or on the ground. Certainly, nobody in authority confronted them, no police or official interveners. I considered checking my email or listening to my office message machine but my cell phone chimed, startling me, if into relief. I picked up, tried to answer. "Hello," I said, but heard nothing, neither the familiar sound of my real voice nor the one in my head. I assumed there was something wrong with the connection, but of course immediately understood rather that there was something wrong with me, something broken or lost or taken or missing.

"Hello?" asked a woman's voice. "Hello. Campus police. Is anybody there?"

No, I thought. Not me, at least. Not here. Not there. Nowhere. Not anybody. And no one to hear, to see, to witness, to object, to speak out, to state the obvious, to myself or, well, who?

The voice on the cell phone continued, the operator from campus police asking if I had just placed a call, and to please identify myself. I desperately, urgently longed to identify myself, to hear myself. I wondered what I might actually say. I struggled mightily to speak, then looked up to see from my office window the arrival of yet another phalanx of believers, this one larger than all of the rest of them combined, its members clad in weird military

100

costumes, exaggerations of martial fear and authority, near-mockeries of dress uniforms if all too, well, sincere. Boots, brimmed hats, belts. They goose-stepped, one row after another, to the rhythm of a drum, carrying lit torches, and bellowing their collective demand loudly, their call to arms chanted in unison, "We want God! We want God! We want God!" Smoke billowed across the quad. One of the leaders, with his evocative short haircut and blunt moustache, his armband and polished boots, spotted me at the window, and pointed. I held my cell phone to the air, hoping the person on the other end might appreciate somehow what was going on, a reflexive gesture, hopeless and mute and desperate, but of course they hung up.

The march outside continued by. I heard hollering and loud steps from the stairwell.

Glass shattered, doors slammed. I ran to the hallway and pulled the fire alarm, then returned to my office to lock the door and wait. I moved my desk to block the door, to slow their entrance but I knew, understood, finally, that when these pretend soldiers came for me at last, there would of course be no one there to protect me, no one left to object, nor to speak for me. And soon there would be, it appeared, no me.

The fire alarm offered its piercing if useless warning. For whom? Too late, misunderstood, general if pointless. It only called attention to the situation, as if reprimanding, chastising me.

There was, it should be noted, uselessly, no one else to alarm, to scold, and no one left to respond to it, nobody left to speak, or to speak out for anybody at all and, besides, there was really nothing left to do or to say, nothing and no one to defend or protect anyway, nothing at all to challenge, nothing even to deny, and lots of it.

for Courtney Lawton

PART 3: INTERMEDIARIES

KEEPING TAHOE BLUE (A NOVELLA)

I SEE NOW, LOOKING BACK, and backwards, with a kind of "moral" or insight offered right here at the start, that we all had our reasons for getting away on that long-short late winter-early spring weekend, from shame, duty, sadness and failure to regret and faith and hope, each the consequence of a modest defeat pretending perhaps to be something else, posing as some kind of stupid mid-life test of insight or of maturity or wisdom. It was just the kind of thing we middle-age cipher-people—stand-ins for some imagined demographic ideal—are supposed to believe that other grownups also know about, endure, but then shrug off as if it were ordinary, expected, even required. I, Otis Clarke, the putative hero or anti-hero of this tale, needed that particular kind of test like I needed a hole in the head, which is to say another hole in my head besides those I'd already received (as one does), most of them unexpected, some self-inflicted, wounds which healed after a while, which closed up and left tiny scars which (we are also promised), might be recalled as somehow instructive later, as object lessons, even as small life- trophies commemorating achievement, success, strength, sagacity of all things! This was quackery, of course, pop sociology, received or accepted non-wisdom, and it reminded me of earlier eras' embrace of Phrenology or trepanation, the former where people who did not know anything about anything at all diagnosed one's skull-bumps as troubles and failings or, the latter, somebody else similarly ignorant nonetheless attempting to stop the pressure inside by drilling a hole, right into the bone of the forehead. Sure, a little skin would eventually grow over the incision but before that happened, lucky thing, anybody could briefly peek inside at the brains—your brains, somebody's brains—for a glimpse at your special home-grown thought-goo, maybe a smidge of it even leaking out just a little, sure, although, in this case, a little, any at all, was probably too, too much.

The real or hypothetical test part aside, and the scars, too, and the potential oozing of precious cerebrospinal brain fluid also, I am fairly sure now that I had not ever really even wanted insight or maturity or wisdom or redemption, thanks. And I certainly did not need to look like a lumpy old colander-head in the meantime, and not with my random gray matter exposed either, or lost, and certainly not on my family-and-friends' shared mini-vacation, not me, a community college English teacher with tenure, a wife and family, albeit a name suggesting both an elevator and a classic American milk chocolate-peanut butter bar, too, and—let's get right to it—an opioid habit which I knew that attempting to break would be an experience involving anxiety, stomach cramps, sleeplessness, crawling (or itching) skin, loss of breath, dizziness, nausea, headache and humiliation or worse.

I had done some reading, as one does these days, surreptitiously, later deleting the "search history" on my PC, the hidden record of a cautiously reasonable bit of casual online research mostly at "AskMD.com." All of its promises were just scary enough to first send me back to denial, then after a few days to try again, this time locating reassurance meant to make withdrawal easier to at least imagine, by which I mean harder to imagine actually achieving, and only to just imagine.

I considered other fates, normal, predictable, non-junkie fates, which seemed to be what other people's mid-life tests promised, along with less dramatic if depressing side-effects: hair loss, weight gain, impotence, insomnia, night sweats, impotence, cancer and worse, and was grateful, weirdly, for my own pathology. But I also wondered why my life-challenge, despite being completely self-manufactured, couldn't have been something else, maybe something a lot easier, like running a 10k or a test of my skill reciting state capitols or naming all the U.S. presidents in order, World Series-winning teams or lists of homophones, air and heir, vain and vein, all of which I used to be able to do so easily long ago, when I was a boy of twelve, my twin sons' ages actually.

Yes, you will see that I was (and am) subject to flights of fancy and, you can see already, I was probably being much too easy on myself, but then I crash landed, if gently enough, my flight interrupted, so that nobody noticed, not really. I'd walk away, uninjured, from the accident that was, it seemed, both me and what was happening to me, staggering but unhurt, a little bruised but a normal-enough seeming guy, high-functioning as they say. Usually, to further abuse the metaphorical (get used to it) I seemed to land in water, with sea plane-style good luck and swim to shore. I surmise now, big picture-wise, that even as a kid, I was already falling, diving into, belly flopping, swimming along in the natural human confusion-pool of self-interest and empiricism, two opposing currents in a small lake, a big lake, or perhaps only an Olympic-sized pool, the weird chemistry of cause and effect combined, if with too much chlorine, for clarity, my eyes wide open if stinging later.

Yes, I had always been a good swimmer. I could hold my breath. I remembered kicking hard. I enjoyed being underwater.

Now, a lifetime later, I had not been in the water much, real or metaphorical, and so instead took a careful half of a prescription painkiller as needed, usually by mid-day, usually actually, yes, as in daily, and as a result I felt euphoric and then energized and much better generally and also happily indifferent, in that order, for the latter half of each day, a bit of self- therapy which I of course kept completely secret, with an automatic prescription refill and insurance paying for it all. I was otherwise healthy, fit, and of course profoundly disappointed in myself.

But occasionally your own life conspires with others' lives to challenge you and your duplicitous storytelling, mostly to yourself, about things finally working out someday nonetheless and despite and why not. And perhaps matching a group tale told, affirmed, a live-and-learn shared redemption narrative, a way to get by and even be happy, though in my case lately it was mostly just live, with not much learning.

No doubt the ever-positive constant revision or accommodation was due, finally, to fear of death, or of life, or the evolutionary demand of survival, or so as not to discourage the children, your own children—by which I mean mine—who are making their own way. They were listening, talking to each and other and themselves, taking, yes, swimming lessons or, as my two clever boys, pre-teen existentialists, called them, laughing together hysterically, "not-drowning lessons." (The rotten apples did not fall far from the tree.)

Or maybe there was some other, bigger, unimaginable fear, suddenly easily enough realized in, as it turned out, a gorgeous pristine blue alpine lake in northern California for instance, a national treasure celebrated by all but always threatened by an inexplicable spill, or explained completely by a completely explicable spill, or perhaps the whole premise itself of "lake" and "pristine lake" revealed as completely contrived too, a p-i-l-l buried there, easily, in a s-p-i-l-l, and the real story or test or challenge, with its upside-down, underwater beautiful logic of dream-possibility made impossible, finally, to deny, even by me, Yours Truly or un-truly.

What am I talking about exactly? Fair question! A test, friends, as in a trial, as in an experiment, as in other words, in that other sense of the word, just another chance to fail or succeed or survive or observe, or only recalibrate or, as if anybody needed that, to learn something or learn more or again or this time even better.

The more clumsily vivid if tragically quantifiably and immediate and urgent life-circumstance here beyond my own was my wife Lizbeth's old dad Max dying, for months, then living, and then dying again. To watch his dear only daughter's own health in decline, my beautiful former ex-girl now quickly grown older herself (sometimes in the non-negotiable space of a short half-hour) was to watch time-lapse photography in a perversely harsh old-school high school botany class nature documentary, the tiny sprout growing from a seed out of the soil, stalk developing, its green head rising toward the sun and finally flowering brightly, flourishing, but then, with the harsh ringing of our goddamn telephone once again (off-screen, very loud) or the arrival of medical test results, wilting just as quickly in the now cracked, dry earth for lack of sun or nutrients, water, and maybe other elements, physical or perhaps even metaphysical, all described in what sounded like the deep, mellifluous voice of the PBS *Frontline* narrator. I had lately adopted it as my own inner voice, of trusted companion and life-coach, a job for which I should not of course have hired myself (of all people!) but which, all things considered, I was the only one qualified for, also unqualified for, but finally the only applicant.

As a result, I had come to comfort or assure myself in my own quiet, calming internal talking-to public media voice, summoning up a kind of available catch-all purposefulness-quotient for everything, unbelievable but insistent, a we're working-together balm based on understanding all of it as elemental, something like appreciating those impossible, invisible, undetectable "humours" (not funny) of the Greeks: blood, phlegm, yellow bile and black bile, puzzling stuff indeed, and which science has not yet completely figured out—what were those Greeks thinking? This might have been the Vicodin talking, of course.

Perhaps, I speculated, high and not, what was happening was the result even of just the sound of that terrible telephone ring-tone and not the predictable news itself, or something in the busy motion of air or the density of water, of nanometers or frequencies, absorption or reflection carrying news of the inevitable through solid and gas and liquid and stars. Do I sound a little spacey? Well, then, yes, I do! I was high about six hours a day, after all.

Well, then, to start again: As a result of my father-in-law's slow, unintentionally sadistic (and masochistic) dying I hadn't seen much of my sweet bride lately, though just enough to still pretend. I spoke calmly, softly to her, in that voice I used similar to the confident civic one I heard in my head, a handsome and faithful NPR announcer who tells listeners the time and the name of the network and seems so reliable though of course he or she is thousands of miles away or may even be pre-recorded. I was, it seems, hearing voices. And then mimicking them.

Comfort-wise, to sustain us both we had our enduring memories of one another, after all, of ourselves together as seasoned spouses, domestic partners, participants in a campaign, officials or managers in something like a company. The details of those formal established relationships remained in place despite it all. We paid our utility bills and gassed up the cars and completed our respective days' work as public education instructors at the local community college, she over in the Sciences and me in Humanities, so that we complemented each other and often found plenty to complain about but not actually do too much to object to or challenge: administrators, colleagues, students, the district's elected board, the state of the classrooms, parking, the war, the idiot president. We got flu shots at the nurse's office on campus together, for instance, at the beginning of the semester, and admired the sunsets over red wine when we could, and sorted the recycling with the satisfaction of seeing something settled, even just that. We fed the big potted white and yellow flowered plumeria its special plant food and coffee grinds, and changed the cat's litter box. We contributed monthly to our IRAs without really even knowing it, courtesy of automatic deposit, which was also of course automatic withdrawal, the kind of transactions which seem self-affirming if also self-defeating, not that paying attention changed anything.

We nourished and supported our two boys with car-pool duty, bake sales, piano and guitar lessons and, our handsome twelve-year olds, Lincoln and Darwin (yeah, I know, we don't do much to avoid our stereotypes and, further, to graft them like tiny branches to our own kids) grew only taller in seemingly exaggerated recompense for the assault of time on their parents and grand-dad, with matching outlines of identical faint near-moustaches, I-phone ear buds plugged in, reading twin adventure books about precocious, talented, alienated adolescent children who resembled them albeit with super-magical powers, and both wearing their matching *Doctor Who* sweatshirts.

All of it suggested that the twins were being more completely themselves than were we, if still extremely tentative selves, and also more present somewhere else, away from us and probably better for it, already living a preview of their own promising futures independent of their parents, and taking the dying grandfather in stride, as they should.

Meanwhile, Lizzie was spending spent a lot of her time at the nursing home with her dad. That was, to be honest and also kind of selfish about it, time which had once been our time. At that other home, which was not really a home at all, there faded together if at various different speeds a whole meadow of old human flowers, wilting on their breathing machines, drowning in sluices of weak IV-drip nourishment, sliding along fitfully across the indoor-outdoor carpet on their walkers, with once-bright neon-green tennis balls punctured into renewed if crude functionality and stuck on the ends of their aluminum surrogate legs, or parked in wheelchairs in the lobby, waiting by the automatic glass double doors for a gust of non-air conditioned, unconditioned, warm, fresh, pollen and filthy particulate-rich air or for death or for their grandchildren, whichever came first, or didn't come at all.

When my Liz was not sitting at her own father's uncomfortable bedside there in the dismal east wing of, yes, no kidding, Freedom Village: An Active Retirement Home, she was on the telephone from our own extremely active home, talking with the nurses and administrators and custodial staff of the facility, or checking her email for doctors' directions and messages from insurance people or questions from the pharmacy or updates (a cruel word, not usually "up" at all) from, lately, as in very late, hospice.

Hospice was not really a place, more a team, a physical crew of very good people who visited Max daily and who in their assembly at his bedside constituted, personified, the whole concept of the immediate and the tangible yet somehow it was always "from hospice," as if there were a faraway geographical place near or in-between, a negotiable proximity, an imagined milieu. I suppose there kind of is, was, should be: a moveable limbo-locale not on any map but as real and locatable in its purposefulness as anything, meaning as real, finally, as death itself.

Despite their help, it all was still a full-time job for Liz, and more, watching her father die, though she took a break once in a while just to break down. I would find her about three times a week quietly locked in the downstairs bathroom, retreating there to weep deeply for ten minutes, no more, very economically, brave girl. She emerged restored, eyes dried, face washed, to take care of the rest of us, or so she insisted, to take care of her foolish husband and two perfect dumb handsome smart identical kids, her surviving, even thriving relations, visiting cousins and aunts or uncles, each and all ready to absorb some life and yet be ready once again—as prepared again as one could—for more of the invisible violence of mortality, the loud warning noises before the actual, cruel final whimper of it.

She had for recent months slept never more than two or three hours at a time each night and it was beginning to show despite my lying to her tired face that it did not. She knew this, of course, and confided to me in the hallway outside her tiny weepatorium, where she demanded more than once that I just hold her, please honey, hard and tight, that's all, no talking, no kissing, whispering that she didn't, couldn't even look at herself in the mirror, that she was herself—her very self—gone or lost or disappeared, to which I responded by assuring her of her lively and urgent presence, her beauty and generosity and, lamely, of my own devotion, only reminding somebody of something they really wanted but could not actually have just then, and could not do anything with even if they (she) had it, and as if this were not even more cruelty.

But she seemed to want or even need my weak comfort anyway, and accepted from me this feeble reassurance until we were called to the telephone once again. Occasionally I found this a good time to have a second painkiller, for obvious reasons.

"You should get away, missus," her father's main caregiver suggested, reflexively, professionally if nonetheless sincerely. She was on the speaker phone, too loud, the one in our kitchen, which is where we often assembled. The nice woman had trouble with titles and pronouns, confusing gender, not that it mattered really, and often just picked the plural over the singular, female over male, and just went for it. What did it matter? We were all the same, alone or together, woman or man.

Then Nurse Iris spoke to me in particular, knowing that I must surely be standing there too, which I was, and as if I might have some say here. "Mr. Otis, sir, you need to take her on a make-away, sir."

Flora, one of her dad's earlier caregivers, had also suggested this, before, if less urgently. As it happens, all of his, our, aides to this point had been named after flowers: Daisy, Jasmine, two Rosas. All had been through this before many times, they reminded us, the decline, improvement, convalescence, re-decline, waiting, un-decline, recovery, adjustment and then, well, presumably, the end of it, finally, one way or another.

Now, Iris—originally from Subic Bay—my father-in-law's newest if perhaps, yes, final immigrant Filipina nurse, a woman who was professionally responsible for other people's parents as well as her own back at home, seemed to be confiding in us, telling a secret that was not so secret at all, a tip, the kind of advice you'd read in a travel or lifestyle or home improvement magazine, disregard and then, suddenly, at the right moment recognize as entirely brilliant, appropriate, apt, exactly right after all.

"I seen it many times," she said. And I believed her that she had seen it, whatever "it" was, and all of it, and more. This lovely brown round-faced woman with her own elderly mother and father living far away, who was not especially articulate, spoke not a whole lot of English, and generally offered very little advice at all, of course possessed experience and wisdom and empathy which people who were not professionally ministering to the dying all the time did not have, and of course did not need or want, especially overachievers and responsible daughters as my Lizzy, and others who still imagined that there was an answer, somehow, to whatever it was that was happening here in puzzlingly if predictable and deliberate insistence, answerless.

Indeed, Lizzie had ignored Flora's, and then Iris's advice for so long, and so politely, that it had become a kind of joke with us, the "I seen it" pidgin and calling me "Mister" with my first name, and the taking-making-getting-away mix-up, some kind of beautiful second-language poetic confusing of a make-over and a get-away. Again, it did not matter. Until, when, a moment after Iris hung up, our friend Ruth Sarkissian called and said it too, and loudly, not because of the phone but because she always spoke like that.

"You should just take her away," she advised me, us. "Right away. Now." I suspected some collaboration, even choreography here, and, frankly, welcomed it.

"I know!" she said, elaborating. "We'll all go. We'll take the kids out of school, rent a place together. Now, before..." She didn't need to finish the sentence, but the thing about Ruth is that she could have anyway, honestly, and nobody would have thought less of her, or been hurt because she is just that kind of confident and empathetic deliverer of difficult truths. Sure, even if maybe she had conspired with one of the helpful nurse-blossoms, which I suspected, the timing here was still just perfect.

And so that evening my Lizbeth at last fully heard the suggestion, offered with just the right or new or different inflection, and this time also from her very best friend, maybe a timely warning that things would only, at last, get worse for her and for her father and her family, so that it finally made good sense and she announced right then that she had to, yes, be taken on a make-away.

She was not running from or abandoning her father, she told me quickly, after Ruthie has hung up, as if she needed to confess to somebody, or explain. We returned to the hallway by the bathroom of tears and stood there together again, this time for a completely different reason, the hallway now about taking, finding a way out, if temporarily, and not a retreat or refuge.

Ruthie Sarkissian is indeed can-do and enthusiastic, and she promised that she would go online immediately and arrange it all for Lizzy, for us, best family friends, the way that only Ruthie could, pull the kids out of school on Friday and play more hooky on Monday, rent a van, and make it all work in order to squeeze in a two-family long weekend away, moderately far away but within reach, while there was still a "before," because who knew, she said, when, about anything?

Ruthie was pregnant, once again, very, and herself uncomfortable physically if happy enough, existentially. I was eager to put my wife and myself and my two sons in Ruthie's hands. My recently problematic Composition student evaluations had been a disturbing surprise to me, if only because I'd taken to ignoring them altogether, confidently, carelessly, narcotically, until at the end of the recent winter term, the beginning of what should have been my easy spring quarter, the teaching-free summer break not so far off when you thought about it (and I did), when I'd been reprimanded by the Chair and threatened with formal review and disciplinary action, a hollow threat indeed considering my tenured status and vigorous union representation and everything I personally knew about the Chair, the Dean and the college president, all of which they certainly did not want others to know.

Still, closing the door of his office and yelling at me had been fair enough, I thought, and in letting him just go at me like that for five full minutes without objection I suspect that he knew that I understood the requirement that he perform this official reprimand.

But all I could think was that his office was a real shit-hole, with papers stacked everywhere, each secured with an unlikely, heavy, and apparently found object, an old iron, a cracked purple and white geode, a rusty hammer and a chipped red brick. It all looked like a yard sale or a collection of obscure if life-sized *Monopoly* tokens, each weighing down what amounted to the unperformed task of reading the damn things, memos and reports and scan-tron tests and unread, ungraded student essays, and more student essays.

I had stood there some weeks earlier next to the antique if peeling globe on top of one stack and noticed, as before, that the earth was not covered in water but, once again, covered in dust. And that the carpet of his office featured a path of perfect, tiny mouse turds, and that half the light bulbs were burned out and I started to feel a little ill, just thinking about the Hantavirus which I was breathing in, and allergies, and worse, not to mention the bawling out, justified, at least in some perfect pedagogy administration-world where students were happy because, yes, teachers made them so and were unhappy for the same exact reason.

I sat down on his musty old love seat, a soft, worn thing which consumed me, causing my Chair to seem to assess my posture, partly correctly, accurately, as regretful, beaten, full of regret, regrettable, which it was, sort of anyway, now for one more reason of many, or any, not to mention the weird sofa.

According to the student comments, or at least some of them, I was condescending and bitter and angry, not on students' side, and "completely out of touch with the average American college student," whatever that meant. It seemed I talked too much about the war, or wars. I also made fun of people with whom I did not agree, or so wrote some super-duper observant student, including, said she or he, President Bush of all people (!) and reported that my presumed "ultra-liberal" leanings frightened and angered and "disrespected" some students. This was news to me, not that it was an excuse. In fact, these students' perceptions of me were, it turned out, as important (if not more) than my actual teaching. Or so he said.

I wanted just then, as the Chair shared highlights of these bad reviews, to put my forefinger on a spot on that decades-old globe which sat between us and helpfully obstructed our views of each other and spin it, a flourish which would make me feel better and perhaps also cause everybody else standing just then on the planet, including those students, to fall down.

Yes, those were admittedly rough paraphrases of the comments though, in the case of my presumed out-of-touchness, an actual direct quote from said anonymous student. I did not challenge my out-of-touchness nor did I offer it, alternatively, as a possible asset to my boss, a potentially counterproductive gambit. Nobody else, I had recently concluded, civic-insight wise was it seemed, angry, not about anything. Apparently, everybody absolutely wanted to be in touch with everybody else, except me. So I stood there adjacent the anticipated rotation of the planet and the Hansel and Gretel vermin poop-trail and let my superior do what he was paid, overpaid, to do, which was generous of both of us I thought, and professional and not unkind or overly sadistic and completely in touch.

I would have the next semester, the Chair and I quickly agreed, to work on being liked, of all things, being more in touch, whatever that meant, likeable, to come back from the spring break better able to meet the needs of my students, who needed a nicer teacher, who apparently did not dislike the President, supported the war, and were not liberals, again, whatever that meant. School was for everybody, he reminded me.

Even the teacher?, I wanted to ask.

We had to reach them where they were, he continued, wherever they were, as if reading from a script, as if the students were scattered across some vast geography—the football field, maybe, the parking lot—and not all in a single small classroom.

And where are they again? I wanted to ask. But did not.

We had to make the classroom a safe place, he reminded me, again reciting from the script, and summoning up other bad-attitudinous hypothetical questions from Yours Truly, all immediately suppressed. I concentrated instead of objecting or cracking wise on chewing exactly half of one of the lovely bitter prescriptions painkillers I kept on my person, originally prescribed, I should point out, for Restless Legs Syndrome. I had by then become too reliant on them, timing, as had become my habit (pun intended), my well-concealed self-dosing to best manage getting me through the latter part of the days but this particular day being especially challenging found myself jumping the hydrocodone gun, as it were.

"I mean to say that we have to create a learning environment comfortable to all," the Chair insisted, generously, as I sat uncomfortably there but tasted the hard white powder of relief and courage and contentedness and, yes, comfort (!) dissolve in my precocious and helpful saliva, and so believed him, agreed, happy with the results of the meeting as anyone could be, or at least I could be. That tiny euphoria-bullet to my brain provided its short-term benefit and, probably, I knew full well, long-term damage to my liver, kidneys, spleen, cerebrospinal fluid, whatever, but I was not thinking about that then, only feeling relieved and hopeful, or whatever the term might have been to describe the contrived temporary antidote to my modest crisis, the involuntary kicking at, well, what exactly? What had made my legs, of all things, so restless?

I nodded at him, with him, in my mind already on to the next activity. I had briefly considered quitting, or announcing my early retirement, even feeling sort of pleased with myself (!) by now and affirmed for being, yes, so presumably out of touch with young adults, students who did not seem to know anything about anything, and who did not want to know anything, no thanks, especially if it got in the way of passing a course with a B-plus, which seemed to be exactly what just everybody always wanted, that perfect and meaningless feint, dodge, substitution for a real grade.

But of course I *needed* my actual job, I still believed I liked teaching and was otherwise good at it (with outstanding grades awarded, big numbers in other categories beyond likeability, lots of letters of recommendation written for students who apparently liked me well enough to ask for my recommendation) but did not say that, did not say anything much in fact, and only observed quietly to myself, noting the familiar high, with my mind clouding up and then raining down in the gentle extinguishing of troubles or pain, the tonic seeming to kick in already.

After all, I needed these students, customers or clients, fundamentally, to even be a teacher at all, and I had better shape up, but meanwhile had soon after leaving the meeting ingested the other half of that preciously and carefully divided half-capsule of Vicodin, or a generic for Vicodin—Lortab, Norco, Maxidone, Hycet, Zamicet, Zydone—what's in a name, what the hell, it had been that kind of a day, three weeks ago, the pre-test as it were for what was coming, and soon.

For his part Aris Sarkissian, attorney-at-law, Ruth's devoted husband and my own best friend had, always and enduringly, the 1915 Armenian Genocide to worry about, lucky him, along with the travails of his clients, poor and unemployed and homeless people with impossible grievances against an impossibly rigged system, bosses who'd fired Aris's crippled, poor or single-father or single-mother clients for needing to show up late to work in order to drop a kid first at daycare, or who had taken away a wheelchair ramp, or hired a divorced ex-junkie mom and then insisted that she have her tattoos removed of all things, for which they'd at first promised to pay but then decided halfway through the costly (and painful) laser procedure that she was responsible after all, leaving the woman with only half her laser removal completed, infection, no antibiotics, risk of amputation and then out of a job, fired her, no kidding, real story.

These bosses were the same in all his stories, and their victims, Aris's plaintiff-clients were also all the same in their sad way so that despite the details of each particular case I always held in my mind the image of the same single client, a composite, a Sad Everysack he'd represented, it seemed, for maybe fifteen years now but for whom Tom had yet to obtain justice. I suppose that person had in my mind become Armenian, too, like Aris, Armenian-American, even though the real people he so heroically represented were usually Mexican or Black or Samoan or Hmong, or disabled or old or prostitutes and never probably Armenian at all, not even a little bit, but a whole other kind of historical victim.

I imagined that this was how Aris saw them, too, which made sense, considering the empathy he seemed to be able to generate or summon, infinite and of course impossible, and no doubt tiring. And, yes, he had five little Armenian-American-Jewish-American children, with one more on the way. This was perhaps his further commitment to every and all kinds of human solidarity, the personification of the repopulation of the world, two worlds, lost but coming back like gangbusters, you bet. He'd said as much, and not just joking around. Big responsibility, that. So, yes, that was Aris.

On our first morning in the magnificent rental house on the famous lake, weirdly if pleasingly divided by two invisible state borders drawn somewhere down its center and then doglegging to give more to California, he and I were up early, tired, driven perhaps out of an eagerness to fulfill both husbandly duty and fatherly responsibility, to achieve the easy practical success of starting the first official day of this bespoke mini-vacation just right for our total of seven kids and two wives, exercising moral strength, or maybe seeking some relief or redemption in the simple arrangement of a normal all-American late spring four-night budget getaway at the private rental at the legendary luxury locale in the High Sierra. We might well pay for this demanding physical effort later in the day, collapsing into well-deserved mid-afternoon naps when the sun was at its highest. We'd driven all night to get there, after all, slept only a few hours after unpacking while wives and kids lay conked-out wherever they had fallen, half-conscious, upon arrival, a lovely, privileged sight.

And, having left the painkillers at home, recklessly, on purpose, in a brave if stupid gesture of enforced self-discipline or punishment or rehabilitation completely unsupervised by a medical professional, I sensed already that I was likely kidding myself, would sleep only fitfully if at all, figuring that my heart would soon be racing, skin crawling as promised, and worse, the consequences of my decision, my own dumb little self-test of will or endurance or self-discipline, a perfect storm if on a totally peaceful day at the placid and crystal-clear and blue lake.

We two drank our extra-strong coffees at just before sunrise, barefoot and each wearing our G-movie rated version of daddy nightwear. This costume suggested easy middle-aged public chasteness and time spent at the gym where we swam and played racket ball together. It lacked any real demonstrable physical achievement to speak of, but I liked to believe it kept at bay the forfeit of time: sweatpants and faded, thinning sweatshirts and rumpled undershirts still on from the long night before, one of peaceful modest civil disobedience back home with about a hundred others, typical of Aris in both inspiration and execution.

He'd been eager to set up the house and finish unpacking the giant rental van, to move things into full rest-and-recreation mode but so far we'd managed only to make a vigorous nod in that direction, gear piled everywhere, duffel bags, the contents of two once-full monster ice chests transferred to the big refrigerator, plastic storage boxes of books and toys and clothes stacked at the edges of the massive kitchen counter island. I read clippings and pamphlets assembled in an old-style photo album, news and stories and legends about the lake taken from the local newspaper, including its size and geological history, one a doozy titled "Lake Tahoe Fun Fast Facts," full of both scientific verity and the kind of wonder you sense in amateur nature writing, produced out of local pride, even mild chauvinism, as if the lake were guarded or cared for somehow by the authors themselves, as if it were here for them, could not exist without their stewardship and affirmation, an existential subjectivity evidenced in details on the depth of the lake, its particular hue, its unique species of deep-water native fish. Reading it felt like somebody describing an imagined place, or following one of those calming guided meditations. I felt better as a result.

Inside, Lizzie and Ruth slept undisturbed in their respective bedrooms while the children lay just where we'd left them so very late the night before, only hours ago, early morning actually, the two awkwardly beautiful pre-teen girls in their shared room, still in their clothes, the littler one in bed with her mom. Their two boys lay in their own respective rooms, chosen quickly, but among so many to choose from, and my own two young fellows were wrapped together in a large sleeping bag on the thick dark ugly shag carpet of the main room of the rental house, a mansion we would share for three more nights, or so was the plan. It was a ski chalet right on the north end of the lake, with too-high ceiling beams and extra-large windows and mounted deer, moose and elk heads, all super-sized. There was a rec room with a billiards table, *foosball*, an upholstered bar, arcade games, an old-fashioned barber chair, soda fountain and a juke box, with a long private dock out front, all of it hard to take seriously, this hyperactive embrace of profligate leisure, except that it was all new to our modest and class-conscious children, terrific news indeed, without the critical or political judgments or disdain of adults, kids who would no doubt love every bit of it when they woke up and saw it all, a crazy arcade of abandon, in all its possibility and exhilaration and wild, reckless fun.

Ruthie had found the place online, taken the virtual tour slide show, renting it at the very last minute. All of this was normally beyond our means, not to mention a challenge to good taste and, for lack of a better phrase, cultural preference. It would be fun for the kids and, for us, a comic lesson in how the other half lived or at least vacationed. Because everybody wanted or needed an antique barber chair in their home?

Yet it had been understood by all involved, the owners and we two couples, that the Lizbeth and Otis Clarkes and the Ruth and Aris Sarkissians and their big combined super-brood were doing the owners, Robert and Norma Peck of North Lake Tahoe a favor, paying a significantly reduced rate yet living like sultans during this moment of economic slowdown, crisis, recession, permanent off-season, whatever it was called, and at least "using the place" instead of it just sitting there vacant. Or so said Ruthie, who'd been so good about making this happen—to quote Lizbeth exactly, "Thanks for making this happen"—which is both a clumsy phrase and the acknowledgement of one's own occasional inability to make thing or things happen for one's own self, and gratitude when others do it for you, which is perhaps foreshadowing, even on a bright, sunny day with not a cloud in the sky, what would develop.

Ruthie Sarkissian, frequently pregnant and persistently happy, was disappointed only, it seemed, that my Liz was not. She adored our twins, as she did all kids, and insisted that life needed replenishing by "the good people," meaning us, presumably. It was an honest if conceited, mutually-esteeming bit of self-regard, of targeted, immodest optimism not to mention political commitment and, not to mention further, her complete ignorance about my romance and attempted break-up with hydrocodone bitartrate.

I'd actually had my own self fixed after the birth of the boys, which she knew, a vasectomy not a repair. We'd already had our second child, after all, at the same time as our first, so two kids total, and any further effort in the direction of reproduction would, I'd calculated—and we'd agreed—put us at risk of double trouble once again. But sure, sometimes, especially around the World's Happiest Family, that decision made me a bit sad and wistful, if not too very often. We'd produced our own two Great Kids, as they say, later in life, as they also say, and it was "all good," as the kids themselves said, my own community college students, too, so often that it had almost stopped bothering me, if not quite, this breezy, dumb affirmation or assessment of non-discernment, non-judgment. It was not all good, in fact, it was often all fucked up, and yet nobody bothered to tell kids that, not mine, not the students at the college, not their parents either. Except, it seems, that I had, which is maybe what got me in trouble. Condescending. Cynical. Angry. Hard grader.

I had instead of reproducing further committed to being a default uncle-type to Tom and Ruthie's five children, in addition of course to being at least good enough, responsible, loving parent to my own boys, prone to fierceness and sentimentality, the mild and mostly nearly completely under-control (but not, of course) addiction notwithstanding. But Ruthie was one of those jolly pregnant ladies, which is what she actually called herself, fit and exemplary, who wanted everybody else to be happy and pregnant and alive too, all the time, including Liz and Aris and me, even complete strangers and animals and statues, motor vehicles, trees, for Ruthie in her state (fecund, productive, still procreative at age forty, if likely for her last time) had become omnipotent and irrefutable, beautiful and powerful, the reliable go-to font of completely unreasonable and necessary passion for life, people, politics, the future of the species and the planet itself.

But pregnant or not, Ruth was, as it happened, also often just plain wrong about almost everything of the immediate, and quotidian—directions, cost, dates, size, time, distance—so that I should not have been surprised, none of us should have, at the inevitable misunderstanding with the owners of the chalet, who showed up just forty-eight hours later, on Sunday night at 10:00 PM (instead of Tuesday morning) with trash bags and cleaning supplies, surprised if not disappointed to see us there, pleased at news of the new baby, grateful to me for saving the water and wildlife of the famous if mysterious lake, affirmed in the verity of the body-mind-lake connection though I am of course getting way, way ahead of myself, and everybody else, the prerogative of the confessor perhaps, the supplicant, the healed and grateful.

Meanwhile, sunrise, placid water, gorgeous morning. Aris pulled up photographs on his laptop while the coffee brewed this first early morning, Friday, easily finding the California section of the *Los Angeles Times* on the small screen, of he and I being peacefully arrested the night before, just hours really, with the others at the demonstration. Everybody's four-day/three-night weekend getaway, make-away departure had been a bit late, delayed slightly because the otherwise patient, bored, polite, even amused LAPD ensemble (all earning generous double overtime pay) had taken its sweet, gentle time holding, booking and then finally releasing us, a group of mostly white, educated, upper middle-class perps with their too-familiar annual message—a whole lot of jolly repeat offenders—so that we'd leapt into the magnificent, sturdy, safe twelve-passenger rental van waiting outside the precinct at 11 o'clock, the kids long asleep by the time we hit the Grapevine, Aris and I drinking weak Circle K coffee, taking turns driving, and making it to the bright, icy-cold and fact-filled lake not a whole lot before sun-up, but making it, safely.

And, of course, there she was in photos from the demo, Ruthie, big and beautiful, the exemplary pregnant woman, standing on the sidelines with her home-made sign, fulfilling her mission on behalf of humanity, the obvious and inevitable and right and just choice, the citizen-actor best cast for personification of the struggle, there to remember and insist, a photogenic Jewess married to an Armenian-American and mother to five, with one more on the way, you bet, a perfect challenge to the deniers, to the Turks, the president who could not make it quite official, the misremembered history of the genocide of her husband's, and now her children's ancestors, a one-woman anti-Holocaust baby-making love-machine and spokeswoman for all that was just.

I'd often assured Aris that I admired Ruthie's stubborn, if too-easy, strategy of consistently rearranging reality in her own image, or including herself, and sure enough here she had done it, once again, a figure irresistible to the *Times* photographer. Truth be told, she was a very strong spirit and a pleasing image indeed, and I am sure she knew that everybody, myself included, was a little bit in love with her, if in their shy, respectful way: tall, curly brown hair, sinewy athletic body, a Mediterranean Ashkenazi beauty with green eyes and white teeth and olive hair and cheekbones like a smitten cartographer might construct toward demarcating all the most delicate possibilities of topography.

Despite herself, or because, Ruthie had also been so very lucky to this point (she frequently said so herself), finding Aris the civil rights lawyer to support and encourage her one-woman mission of restoring justice, advancing mutual aid, insisting on a worldview, her worldview, and also able to stay home with their five kids (and counting), cook and bake, see a few clients (she was trained as a psychotherapist, go figure), volunteer at their mildly disabled younger son Natan's elementary school, be on the board of their youngest daughter Sophia's daycare, work at the garden (organic, of course) of the charter school on whose board she also served, be a good friend to many, and organize trips as this one, where we were expected to give in and adopt her overly organized if predictably imprecise, sloppy and busy itinerary. That included, we'd been promised, early big breakfasts of pancakes and eggs and bacon, hikes in the nearby woods, cycling around the lake, and visits to the local Indian arts and crafts museum on the Truckee River, playtime at the beach, perhaps even a fishing or birding trip on the lake, creating three elaborate dinners together and playing old-fashioned board games, taking sunset walks to the old-timey ice cream stand down the busy main highway, a full line-up of recreation and relaxation for a month, not a few days.

"It's how she works," Aris reminded me, as we took in the shimmering flat lake from the sofa, a massive suede sectional where we sat together, and the emerging sun and the tall mountains on the far other side too, and I took my turn at reading the article and admiring the photos.

"And after the baby's here she'll see more babies just everywhere, and more new parents, and we'll all be the better for it, Otis."

"Because," I agreed, recreating a conversation we'd had before, a dramatic dialogue between two handsome, extremely winning and universally empathetic characters who so closely resembled us, "all of those parents will be good parents. Like her. Like you. Like us."

I reached over and patted my old buddy Aris on the back. We both laughed. I was mimicking myself, and my actions, too, and him, and congratulating and elevating us and taking us both down at the same time, in a cartoon if genuine synchronicity. It was fun, and arch, and sounded like dialog from a TV series about people who were all too aware of how they sounded, and so just went with it. This was something I often did with Aris, brotherly and affirming, for both of us, but also self-conscious. We were close like that, had been since college.

In fact, the night before I'd also reached across the vast front seat of the rental van, again to pat him on the back, offering courage and also making real sure he was not falling asleep at the wheel. The same gestures, offered between friends, could communicate so many different messages. He had nodded vigorously, straightening his posture, coaxing the big twelve-passenger behemoth along. His confidence and strength seemed to actually move us faster, safer, no kidding. And so we had drunk our tall terrible coffees in their limp Styrofoam and I'd turned up the AM radio to see if we'd hear the all-news station reporting, again, on the protest at the Consulate of the Republic of Turkey at the corner of Wilshire and Crescent Heights. It was at first only the usual traffic, sports and weather, especially irrelevant for us, already halfway on our way to Sacramento but then arrived, with a short piece about the protesters, Ruthie of course laying out the argument for an apology, reparations, a truth and reconciliation process and then, briefly, Lizzy answering the reporter's too-easy but predictable question about the riot of children surrounding her, and gently deflecting his too-easy implied concern about the appropriateness of bringing kids. "Where else should my kids be, our kids be, but here, with their parents?"

"Listen to them," I'd said. "We are two lucky dudes, Aris. For all sorts of reasons."

I sounded like a pretty darn satisfied middle-aged guy, and hearing myself, I felt like one too, noting no negative consequences as I could detect, not yet, of my decision to abandon the opiates, still of course much too early for the withdrawal I knew just had to be on its way. I grabbed some bravery and confidence while I could, in other words faking it, before I might really have to fake it. "Go Team Clarke," I was now saying, thinking, to myself, offering the resolve and encouragement and assurance so singularly available to a passenger at night in a fast-moving vehicle with the ghostly trees and distant silhouettes of foothills, the moon, and the highway signs.

Aris put in his favorite CD after the jolly reportorial affirmation from KFWB All-News Radio, and we sang along, quietly, for the five hundredth time, to his absolutely favorite song, Bruce Cockburn's "If I Had a Rocket Launcher," possibly the most frighteningly angry if righteous anthem ever written about wanting to protect innocent people from very bad people, combining vengeance and goodness in a pleasing late 1970's power-rock rhythm.

"If I had a rocket launcher, some son-of-a-bitch would die," we repeated together, at the Turks and the Nazis and all the bad people, and also the good people left behind us too, in Los Angeles or in history or in offices or wherever those other people were on a late Thursday night, early Friday morning, with our own families sleeping in the comfort and safety of nighttime and in the smooth, lucky remove of a moment of satisfaction shared, ours.

And after our morning coffee, we walked to the end of the dock each carrying one end of one of the best of the Peck's small fleet of expensive, shiny aluminum canoes, filled with oars, wet suits, float toys, vests, sun screen, and I said it again.

"Aris," I said, "old buddy, old pal," taking in the lake together, the mountains, the sky, the sun. "Look at this. Now, again. Everybody! Listen up! We are indeed two very lucky radical dudes." I also spoke simultaneously to an invisible audience, a whole world of observers of our precious good luck, not actually present but somehow involved. Bluffing, of course, if also sincere, and scared, but it felt good both ways, with me getting temporarily less curious about going cold turkey and increasingly more afraid, sunshine and clear water and my bravado notwithstanding. The coffee would have helped somehow, or so I imagined, pretended. Should have helped. What did I know about chemistry or addiction or withdrawal, finally? I figured I had about ten, fifteen hours, maybe until that night, before whatever pain arrived to punish me by way of violent, painful withdrawal and when, maybe, I could drink it away, drown it in alcohol (plenty of that in the chalet's bar) and perhaps fall into a different kind of dependency, temporarily, transitionally, as needed, a stupor or more ordinary kind of transgression.

And when we came back inside to check on our families, to survey further the house with its acres of deep-ugly shag carpet and an armada of love seats, sofas, compartment seating to accommodate dozens, perhaps hundreds, we observed my twins on the floor, I could tell by the general outlines, each trying simultaneously to wiggle, to wriggle, out of their too-big adult sleeping bags, yawning and moaning their respective ways into consciousness, squirming to escape, like cocooned creatures metamorphizing into a new stage of their development, if beautifully, completely oblivious to their actions or, more accurately, what was happening to them, being acted upon them, forces beyond their control if, in their cases, a good thing.

It was actually still barely springtime in the mountains, upon which there was very little snow anyway, and cool out, notwithstanding the brightening sun, the brilliant reflection of it on the flat, diamond clear-blue water. The proximity of all that lake right next to us, the night sky dissipating slowly into paleness, the hugeness of the house, the luxury and space of all of it together seemed to invite us into an anonymous zone or ecology of privilege, available to whomever might grab it, and I swore to myself that I could take whatever the pill-lessness could dish out, do better at work, try harder with students, support my Lizzy, be a best-better friend to Aris, from whom I had in fact hidden my junior-junkie habit, follow direction from a generous person as Ruthie, father those boys with love and confidence, be a solid husband, commit further Gandhian civil disobedience if invited, be a witness and truth-teller and be counted on by others in a pinch.

And in the success of the morning so far—media affirmation, funny kids, pristine surroundings, excellent flapjacks produced in huge piles by the two dads, me only slightly manic, mostly anticipatory, if still scared—I saw exemplary events or circumstances around which to organize expectations for the rest of our weekend. I concluded that I had started off on the right foot and hoped again, quietly to myself, that tonight, if I drank a whole lot of water, took a brisk walk, did some vigorous stretching, sat in a hot bath, maybe even took a sleeping pill or two or three, drank a lot of scotch, retreated to the indoor sauna or Jacuzzi as needed, performed some push-ups, I would not have to struggle so much with the return of the exaggerated symptoms of either my out-of-control knees and feet, which had pre-prescription wiggled and twitched and typically kept me awake for what seemed like hours before I settled down, an exhausted marionette—in other words the condition for which the pills had originally been meant—or endure whatever anxiety, palpitations, sweats—who knew, not me except from books and TV—that kicking narcotics had to offer.

So, no sleep for me that morning, no. After breakfast at around noon, "the girls"—by which we meant, joshingly, our wives—had gotten up and they and the actual girls, the young women and also boys—three Sarkissian girls, two boys, and our two little men—had joined us completely. They'd all found their way to the edges of the dock and into the shade of its boathouse, children and dads jumping in the lake, tossing Frisbees to intentionally necessitate an acrobatic clown leap into the water, the usual exuberance of outdoor freedom. The water was cold, hard, exhausting, somehow right for elevation six thousand feet, with the air thinner than home. Ruthie sat, after a short session of gentle pregnancy yoga, resting in a sturdy plastic Adirondack chair with a footstool. She nodded to passersby, swimmers, families in canoes and in kayaks, in boats, owning the place. She rubbed her big exposed belly in the sun and smiled and whispered to whoever was near—mostly Liz—that there sure were a lot of pregnant women here, weren't there? I had not been paying attention, not really, but had not seen any at all, not so far, not one. I made a note to ask my wife if Ruthie was projecting again as part of her missionary work or could somehow see pregnancy in others, or just see further, or was only performing that gorgeous solipsistic life-affirming behavior of hers.

Still, it appeared there was more than enough affirmation, evidence, and collective assurance that the universe was alive and beating, and I was just as pleased as punch to see it carrying its future in Ruthie. And if the joy and responsibility of it were overwhelming and to be embraced, celebrated, then I would sign on for that kind of overwhelm.

And perhaps it was indeed a good thing to see the world so fecund and promising, especially in this wonderful place with these particular ambassadors of generosity and empathy, whom you could trust. I felt relaxed, if cautiously, of course. We were used to Ruth and Aris after all, and we accommodated them, and they put up with us, too. Aris had pretty much expected me to come along, counted on me to join him at the annual Turkish Embassy protest once again, International Day of Remembrance, April 24, and although I was in no mood, I had, and was once again glad for it, or at least relieved. Compared to other symbolic moral or political stands against evil, this one was pretty darn easy, and low-risk. No counter-protesters, and the cops had been so nice. Maybe that practical reality, the low stakes and yet satisfying moral stance, had also inspired me to go clean, despite the fact that the drug had worked so very well till then, especially when used not at all for RLS but the other syndromes and challenges and tests and trials which a person (well, me) might encounter or construct.

Perhaps I'd imagined I could attach my own modest bit of redemption or liberation to this irresponsible and even reckless gesture, either finding or losing myself in the history of history, of modest history-making, in the talking back to easy excuses, in a crowd where I might be ignored but also celebrated, if by nobody, finally, but myself, and so be unnoticed at a crisis moment when I might otherwise be pitied, accused, held accountable, busted.

Yes, the protest had been easy enough. Who, after all, among the political actors out there in our strange, big world, would interrupt or object to a careful bit of casual street theater organized to defend the long-ago if never-ending murder of Armenians on a Thursday evening? Apparently not even the local Turkish nationalists and Ottoman Empire apologists could summon the bravado to come out against us this year, and the police knew many from the group from previous years so were ready, over-represented, and confident. The atmosphere had actually been festive, fun, with children singing on the sidelines and supporters cupping candles in small Dixie cups and a few priests and imams and rabbis and pastors chanting or swinging their respective miters and crosses and other helpful accoutrements of faith.

Later that early afternoon sitting, drying in the warm air post-laps, still unable to sleep but feeling calmer now on the long, perfect private dock, I considered the smudges of black ink still on my fingers, left there from the previous night's booking. The sun was bright and, anxiety or not, I fell suddenly into a deep dream, still completely awake, or so I imagined, yet so appreciative of the nap I had indeed hoped might indeed sneak up on me, a health-propelling booster against what no doubt lay ahead. In my undream, I narrated a new and welcome story where regret and happiness were—at last!—exactly one in the same thing, reconciled finally in that way that is entirely possible in restorative, beautiful actual dreams with REM-sleep, no logic, no physics, no gravity, no contradictions, just the ease of my healing-itself mind, tying up loose ends, allowing to happen in my unconscious life what I could not permit or accomplish in my conscious one. As if I were a docent in somebody else's dream, as if my own willpower might direct, or redirect what harsh recompense were on its way.

Here in the dream the baby earlier inside Ruthie Sarkissian had just been born but immediately grown too large, into a jolly monster, a big out-of-control Godzilla-child, having big baby fun, stomping and destroying its way through the previous night's protest, knocking down Armenians, reporters, law enforcement, smashing vehicles up and down the 5, Los Angeles to the High Sierra. And yet it was a cute enough baby, a nice baby, if also a disaster. I was again the reporter or host of a PBS-style documentary and went on, or somebody like me, in the style of the narrator of *Frontline*: "A big baby like this one demanded big answers indeed."

The voice of the dream (me) spoke like that, in elaborately comforting affirmation followed by doubt, on the one hand versus on the other hand. I liked him, this familiar-seeming dream guide, and I hoped not to awake, though the real me sensed that understanding the situation as so obviously contrived meant I'd probably be waking up pretty darn soon, my brain coaxing me back, too bad.

Besides, he was me, after all, this alter ego, if so much better than me, and not only asked but helpfully, authoritatively answered all questions and concerns—probably, who knew?—and when I did suddenly wake, startled, to the sound of a child laughing—normal-sized, Sara Sarkissian it was—and the lapping of small wavelets against the side of the dock, and the screeching of a gull, I understood the instructive equilibrium-effort of dream, realigning and struggling to make its sense of things. I also felt at least a bit rested, and grateful for that. I concluded that I must have indeed actually been asleep, if only for a few minutes, enveloped in biological grace, the coffee rush and the long night of driving and the vigorous swim-play in the cold, perfect lake water causing me to crash, momentarily, a small crash, nobody hurt.

Conscious for real, I confronted the mildly confusing developments which had occurred in my brief absence, or super-intense alternative presence. So much had happened, however small. And so the sun shone just brighter, the dock now rearranged in a scattered crazy quilt of obscenely bright oversized beach towels, each with their respective larger-than-life character square: Sponge-Bob, Mickey, Hello Kitty!, the canon of official corporate cartoon imagination. The big aluminum canoe was missing, toys and dive masks, snorkels, fins, beach balls, bright pink picnic lunches strewn everywhere. The loud, frustrated hungry gull sat perched just above me on the railing. A dozen Canada geese floated just below the dock. I sat up. From my vantage, I heard a conversation about squirrels, echoing across the water. The boys, our boys, theirs, or some combination of boys had, it seemed, found a lost baby squirrel at the water's edge and put it in something resembling a shoe box, ignoring the prohibitions, warnings, common sense objections to kidnapping or adopting a wild feral creature which I hoped, expected, assumed some other responsible parent or adult had by now offered. And, yes, I then saw Aris too, supervising, cautioning. Or just letting them, exercising the funny idea that if a grown-up were present or near, that safety would be assured and that the behavior would be protected.

I momentarily thought that I might still be in my fake-o dreamland when one of the older girls, Adrine, called for Liz from the living room, saying she was wanted on the telephone. Uh-oh. I stood up and looked around for Lizzy, finding her out on the water, rowing the canoe with Ruthie 200 yards out, the lake seeming to hold the two of them up, higher somehow than they really should have been. I guessed it was the angle, of seeing them from the dock, and the glare on the water, somewhat blinding me.

I walked inside to get the telephone myself, staggering past Sara, and making a show of my grogginess for Adrine, the dark-haired beauty, nodded and mumbled on my way "Hello, dear," to one of the massive bucks mounted on the wall, as if pantomime and humor might obscure or postpone or somehow help what I knew was about to unfold.

I took the telephone from Adrine, a smart, skinny, pretty girl who reciprocated with a requisite chuckle at my mugging at the big dead head. She is sweet and has the good looks of both her parents, and the quiet confidence of her father. I decided to let her witness this.

It was Nurse Iris the caregiver on the phone, of course—who else?— telling me that my father-in-law Max had died. "Passed," she said. I listened to the predictable details.

What an odd word. Passed. Or was it past?

"Thank you," I responded, automatically. "Is there anything I should do?" I asked her, stupidly.

"Not yet," Iris said, which was both fair and also a funny enough thing to say about death. She explained about the removal of the body and shared her sympathy and apologized for interrupting our vacation, which of course it was not really, not ever, not that I corrected her. I thanked her again, grateful for the promise of exercising some future, better prepared response, and said we would of course call her back and that we would be fine, which seemed both everything you could do and not very much at all. In my mind's eyes I saw my wife and her best friend sitting together in the canoe on the lake, where they were safe, far enough away to still not know. Then I put down the phone. My actual, physical eyes had adjusted to being indoors, and then my mind's-eye followed.

Sometimes it is important to see exactly where you are, in order to consider how to proceed. I considered that big, dead twelve-point buck, the tall beamed ceilings, the two thin beautiful Jewish-Armenian girl-women now standing side-by-side near me the way people do after somebody has taken what is obviously a revelatory call, if one totally expected. I did not want to, but knew I could not stay here in this privileged moment and place, and that I would need to report the news to the grown-ups but for the moment it was just mine and Adrine's and Sara's, and I felt something powerful and quiet.

"Max?" Adrine asked.

I nodded. "I'm afraid so," I said. But, lo, I was not afraid. Both little girls came over, hugged me, and for a long time, and sincerely, too, spreading themselves around my torso with their short, thin arms, generously and yet easily for very young people on whom death has not yet even close to a grip. They were well-behaved and good sweet girls and I thought that I could do anything for them, not that there was much to do.

I looked out onto the dock and past it, and into the glare of the sun and from there saw both mothers for real this time, and could all too easily discern the difference from inside and outdoors, which was something to reconcile, a photo negative, an imprint, a burnishing on the small screen at the back of my eye cavity versus the gentle colors of late April on the tranquil perfect water.

I would like to argue here that somebody, somewhere had anticipated all of this, the Chamber of Commerce or the State or the brave defenders of the famous deep, clear, blue lake, the authors of the informational pamphlets, the discernment and the disconnect and the irreconcilable distance in terrestrial and nautical feet or yards from my dead father-in-law lying still-warm in his hospice bed at the Village of Freedom out through me and the massive living room past the long dock to the two women drifting in the canoe beyond the reach of death or doing anything about it.

Not me, however, and certainly not in these particular details, and certainly not in what followed, including my response. Not as I saw it perfectly just then, immediately, not in the enormous natural amphitheater of clear alpine freshwater sea and not twelve feet below, in the perfect sand, in the thin plume of threatening flat white which the situation of my own foolish self-test allowed me to apprehend before others, and not in the further difficult if welcome revelations about the lake and its caretakers and conspirators, both secret and public, creators and propagators of that ambitious and world-renowned mind-body campaign announced in the famous bumper sticker with the outline of the body of water, which you saw everywhere across the entire state, in small towns and in big cities, north to south, ocean to desert, Keep Tahoe Blue.

But Aris, whose work had regularly caused him much anxiety, whose partners at the firm caused him too much anxiety, whose entire relationship to obligation had recently necessitated counseling and time off of work and some heretofore unimaginable concessions to the maintenance of his mental health or, rather, struggle against mental illness, all "work-related," had been reading and learning to use a self-help technique, a kind of hyperbolic hopeful association-making which now kept him sane and constant, he told me, regardless of whether any of it actually added up to anything, which did not seem to matter.

Knowing about my own problem, my own psychosomatic or anxiety-based physical manifestation, if not the sorry details of my political fuckuptitude with college essay-writing students, and the neurological-metaphorical leg spasms for which my doctor had prescribed the so-lovely drug, just then quite popular with millions of Americans, Aris had tried enlisting me in his effort to locate in me, his project, that same connection (anti-conspiracy, he called it) and to free me, himself and all of us by breathing and meditation and yoga and a good diet, running, playing racket ball, performing honorable deeds and, finally, employing sheer force of will.

He was obviously a better person than me. His body had once armored itself, he said, as had mine, as had everyone's. No, the Armenian Genocide did not help matters. Or the Holocaust either. Or the war in Iraq. Our bodies, his and mine and yours and everybody's, he'd again explained to me after I'd taken over at the wheel the night before, somewhere north and east of Stockton, had responded to generalized and specific and political and worldwide trauma by physically building its weakness-grip into our skeletons, where it just did not belong, no, and which now potentially caused us, like crippled, arthritic knights in armor or the rusty Tin Man, to walk funny, endure back pain, and, for instance, not be able to fall asleep at night due to twitching, kicking and fussing, for instance, and to occasionally wake up in the thin, dark hours with an anxiety attack.

He had himself eschewed drug therapy. Aris and his therapist had together created and installed in his mind an available image, a self-image the therapist called it, to battle against and destroy the heavy armor, thus revealing the strong, lithe, beautiful naked true human. This was romantic and enviable stuff, and I liked it fine. It was facilitated through employment of an imaginary mind-transforming metaphor-gizmo that could take out with comic-book style the dinosaur-like plating of the physique and the brain, or the steel-clad *Merrimac*, whichever, dinosaurs made extinct and the famous armed vessel now sunken in the muddy depths of one's own Potomac at the Battle of Hampton Roads.

There were other historical and apocryphal examples, all terrifically helpful but having such stand-in images doing battle, struggle, resolution in one's head was key to the whole project, the therapy, or so he said.

Those images of one's hero-costumed Self, in this case versions of Aris himself, would be summoned, raised up as needed, anytime, anywhere, in advance or in response to despair, say, and then be retired, so that Aris could feel better, whether about his clients or the innocents lost to battle or, by extension, some hurt he'd sustained and, impossibly, forgotten somehow, this good, good man who always wanted to be better and was or was not.

And what pathological construction, or destruction, I wondered, had existed in my own Restless Legs Syndrome, in the jerking from my knees to my toes? What catastrophe could I discover or locate or identify or invent or imagine toward diagnosing whatever was really ailing me, if anything at all? The Battle of the Little Big Horn, San Francisco Earthquake, Dred Scott Case, the Kennedy assassination, 9-11? Or something less dramatic, like a dying father-in-law, an emotionally exhausted wife, bad teaching reviews, a tendency to assume others shared my worldview—incorrectly!—and the inevitable and disappointing quantification of the time one had left to live? And what counter-strategy or helpful metaphorical device might I adopt, what felicitous answer to the test, testing, testiness which confronted me? Test, as in diagnostic or, yes, test as in critical evaluation or test, as in basis for evaluation or judgment?

And so Max was dead, just like that, only so much more slowly, at age eighty-three. Finally, I thought. Long-distance, I thought. Good-bye, Max.

Adios. Bon voyage. I did the easy math on him on my way back outside, slowly, organizing his final actuarial report, some weird summing of things up for a guy who, yes, I'd kind of resented for the past few years for the tortured arithmetic of patience and anxiety he'd thrust on Lizzy. I guess that the quotidian was about the only way I had not yet considered him, us, the two of them, and here it was, crudely.

I stood in the entranceway of the main room of the weird alpine mansion, and I of course missed him already, and felt it. He was, after all, my beloved's own father, my kids' grandpa, a fine and good person all his own, set upon by his own body, its betrayal or only end result and now was gone, and I confess I was relieved and grateful to him, finally.

Then, there at the end of the long dock stood the Sarkissian's youngest girl alone, Sophia, age seven, pointing at the water and repeating "Look, Uncle Otis, look." She is a child, if a bright, quiet child, and one responds to what they, little kids, see and point to with a misplaced adult confidence, disinclination to be surprised or alarmed. On the other hand, there were kids everywhere around us if none standing with her so, naturally, I imagined one of them drowning, or drowned below, though I had in my dream already glimpsed at its edges an image of exactly what she'd actually discovered, despite having until now forgotten or disregarded it, as happens too often with a dream.

She waved for me to hurry out, the adult in charge.

There," she said, before I even got to her. "Look. See. There. It's nothing. It's all gone."

Between us and the two distant moms, just a few yards from the end of the dock, I saw the thin plume arranging itself, rearranging, articulating its ominous and perfect shape. It had spread after a few yards, transformed from a thin spidery line coming from the bottom of the lake to a cloudy mass to a tinting mixture to flat absence, no other way to say it.

White, after all, is a color without color, a combined, balanced cooperation of all spectra of light-making. I had read that in the pamphlet only hours earlier, and recalled them. As against the blue, it had reviewed helpfully, with its short wavelength, primary power, particles scattered by water, reflecting the high and much-favored California and Nevada sky. I filled in the rest. This was a completely "achromatic" leak or spill, an erasure, obvious and obviously dangerous and frightening even—or especially—to a little girl.

But I recognized it. And what was in it, which was, yes, absolute nothing.

Nothing, indeed, and more. Nothingness. I sensed right there in front of me the active conditions of an undeniable experiment, something like the dream from which I'd just awakened, but more closely connected to me personally, of all people, and my secret, my weakness, my tests.

I recalled further the elements of the helpful Lake Tahoe pamphlet. The body of water, yes, body, is one hundred ninety-one square miles and holds thirty-nine trillion gallons of water fed by sixty-three tributaries, and snowmelt in healthy winters. Its maximum depth is 1,645 feet. For decades the state and residents and visitors and boaters have tried to keep it all clean and clear. The water was 99.994% percent pure. By comparison, commercially distilled water was 99.998% pure.

Imagine that, I had thought, as if a comparison were necessary or even desirable. And, finally, my favorite detail, that this clarity was determined by measuring water depth where an eight-inch diameter white disk, lowered into the depths, disappears from view, an occasion or exercise which I could just imagine, the disk tethered to a line, a boatload of trained technicians staring, as was I now, into the lake to record how long it would take not to see.

The otherwise clear-blue Tahoe water, the sandy bottom of the lake visible here, now, had in this way begun, however small, to turn to a larger and brighter and murderous blank absence—beyond white, destroying not only visibility and clarity but also dimension and perception, hope and time, the unfriendly bright non-color of blindness, of non-dimensionality, thick and chemical as gone-off flat white oil paint, as if it were old-fashioned typewriter White-Out and also the sheet now covering the dead body of Max and, of course, finally, the familiar hue of the small scored pill, if missing only its identifying tiny red dots.

I looked around, nodding at little Sophia. The trickle of deathly un-color coming up from the bottom, growing as it spread, became gradually more menacing. It settled near the surface in a wider-growing circle, a few feet across, a sheen of active absorption of all colors. It threatened in each spreading millimeter the deliberate further absenting, and more death and loss, loss, loss, as if the surrounding scene—of remaining clear-blue water, little girl, fat Canada geese, dock, gull, boys playing on the beach, clear sky and its reflection, moored boats, kayakers, mothers in the canoe—would be overtaken, anything touched by the reverse reverse-osmosis impossible to exist, finally, in this paint-over of all that existed around it.

"Now, it's really making things disappear, Otis" offered Sophia, appreciating the thing's intent. "What is it?" she asked. "I'm scared."

She took my hand.

"Can you do something?" she asked.

A septic tank, a broken buried pipe, I pretended to think, pretended not to think, aiming for the practical, the immediate notwithstanding the larger, clumsily existential challenge. I struggled to come up with an explanation. An abandoned and forgotten underground chemical storage space of some kind? No. What could it be except, of course, that it suggested nothing more closely at its origin point than the shape and familiar form, the emanation of the mind-obliterating chemical tonic of my own small happy-pill, my effort at autonomy and liberation from it here realized in neural shape-shifting and penetration of the natural world, the ultimate in what the poets called the pathetic fallacy, sure, but also perhaps an EPA toxic disaster, and worse. It did not matter which, or both.

"I can do something," I said to Sara. "I will," I heard myself say, both doubting and knowing, apprehending and appreciating my course of action.

That tiny hole in the sand from which the erasing-action effused was nearly if not yet quite obscured by what rushed out of it, an orgy of particle symmetry, matter and anti-matter reconciled. All elements corresponded. People and animals communicated, or only cooperated. An electric current of awareness inhabited the area. So I perceived the moment.

I heard Aris shouting from the shore, saw another man running out onto his adjacent dock a few hundred yards along the beach, an emergency siren starting up in the distance. A dog barked. The visceral response of humans in charge was palpable, immediate, and I sensed that others were as alarmed as were Sophia and I, the threat recognized like a wildfire or flood or earthquake, the players responding after so many previous sirens, tests, emergency practices, drills, this the real deal, all of it realized now through some telepathic herald, absent speech.

I did not have time to further separate or distinguish cause and effect, not now, and of course wondered if I ever had. I saw what had to be done, and that I would do it, without involving any others, without calling further attention or notice. The moment, artificially extended, offered itself. This opportunity, seemingly created by my own previous hours, days, weeks of self-deception, duplicity, dream, of inaction, was undeniable and available. I was here now. I was ready.

"Wait here, honey," I told Sophia. She sat down obediently on a Little Mermaid towel, and in this gesture of childish faith and trust I found further courage and assent.

I stripped to my shorts, grabbed and quickly strapped on a kiddie dive mask there in the jumble of gear and fell right in, gasping only slightly at the cold. I separated the water in front of me with my arms, impressed with my powerful stroke. I kicked. The hole was small, narrow—twelve, fifteen feet down—and I was at it quickly, so obvious as the source, as if in a cartoon drawing of a leak or a wound. You must trust me that this all made sense, the tiny absence I had myself created in the world, the counter-argument and many variables, and now, here, the near-taste of this perverse fountain of decimating toxic fluid just within reach, though I admit I was briefly frightened to actually touch it much less risk swallowing or ingesting it.

There, lying, holding myself really, on the bottom, I watched the life-erasing, hope-destroying liquid slowly seep out and up, glanced at it above me as it gathered at the surface, feeling horrified yet also exhilarated. I saw nothing at all, only the exact perfect blankness of the leak or the spill, nothing in the layer of it on the surface, no sky or sun or shadows, no dimension or depth or even darkness, only a frightening lack, absence, obliteration, perhaps the saddest I or anybody had ever encountered, this manifestation contrived by who, what, to intrude upon the beauty and fullness and possibility of the natural world.

Out of breath, I surfaced, breathed deeply, glanced around at an approaching Zodiac, at Aris shouting and running down the dock, at a still-distant patrol boat with its blinking light on, and little curly-haired Sophia, sitting with her arms calmly crossed around her knees.

On the shore a small crowd had gathered, grown-ups joining the squirrel-boys, the crisis otherwise imperceptible, unnoticeable, unknowledgeable but something definitely up. They seemed to appreciate the emergency, sensing what was at stake. And so I took another deep breath and went down again, quickly finding the aperture in the clean, light-brown sand, just a few inches across, something like a tiny animal air-shaft, a worm-hole, reaching the fingers of my left hand in to plug up the cavity. This action stopped the flow of the scourge, restoring the immediate area to clarity almost at once. I looked around for a rock, my hand anchoring me, finding none. The bottom was, alas, a pristine sand desert, yards and perhaps miles of gorgeous barren perfect landscape.

With my free hand, I pulled off the mask, the only object I had to work with. My vision blurred, my fingers guiding me, I jammed the dive mask into the hole as I removed my fingers, my hand, buried to the wrist. It stayed, it held. The flow stopped, the mask filled, the blank white outline of a half-face staring at me. Nearly out of breath, I smoothed the spot over with sand and, dizzy and gasping, shot up to the surface, light-headed and gasping, coughing but exhilarated. Sophia stood, smiling, clapping, Aris with her now, at her side. He signaled to the old dude in his approaching inflatable, giving him an A-Okay, and seemed to wave off the other approaching craft, which I took upon closer inspection for the Coast Guard. The old fellow in the Zodiac nodded back, waved and immediately turned around. The big motorboat patrol similarly turned back, its pilot not bothering to check further. The dog on the beach stopped barking, the gull flew off, and the two mothers arrived at the dock, asking what the matter was and why I didn't have on a bathing suit, honey.

"Nothing. All good," said Aris. "Fine." Somehow, they knew not to ask, not to inquire further, each it seemed enrolled in the quite, collective civil defense team of which I had been till then the one member available, on the scene, prepared, ready if largely still unaware of the size and scope of the operation. But how often, I wanted to ask somebody, did this sort of thing occur? How lucky had we been? How accidental or serendipitous had my moment been, of redemption or rescue? But I did not, sensing instead that none of this would be spoken of, could be spoken about, not ever. It was impossible to reconcile except that it had been in every way the most perfect arrangement, coordination of need and opportunity, skill and desire, circumstance and, of course, wishful thinking realized.

"Good going," said Aris, patting me on the back and offering me a towel. And so, standing there shivering, wrapped like Dorothy Lamour in my wet, sagging undies and superhero beach-towel sarong, I helped the wives out of their vessel and took Lizzy in my arms, forcing her gently into the little chamber which I hoped, imagined, I had constructed with my damp, cold, invigorated body where she would hear, understand, what had to be reported, gently, just to her for the moment though now I assumed that everybody, everywhere already knew, about just everything.

You already know, of course, that Ruthie gave birth at the hospital, a small walk-in clinic really, in Truckee, less than an hour later, two weeks prematurely but easily enough, as expected. A healthy child, a boy. She might as well have delivered outside on the deck or, inside, on one of the humongous sofas in the massive main room, so easy and effortless she made the whole effort seem. With the arrival of the child, Life had done its clichéd best to challenge Death, helpfully demanding something other, something else from my Lizzy than only grief for her dad. Great timing.

She accompanied Ruth to the clinic, both of them doing that funny slow breathing on the way, a coach and an athlete, with Aris driving and me left with the kids in the messy rental mansion.

Saturday was more playing in-between long stretches at the hospital admiring the newborn, delivering meals to Ruth and Liz and, yes, Sunday night after dinner, the Pecks arrived, surprised to find us all there, except for Ruthie and the newborn still in the two-bed makeshift Maternity Ward, all the lights in the chalet on, clothes and toys and gear scattered everywhere, the house a fun, easy disaster, sloppy spaghetti dinner made with jarred sauce served on paper plates and spiced, buttered supermarket garlic bread in tin foil, the kids Skyping back and forth with the hospital by now, the whole place a bright lantern reflecting its clumsy, absurd, artificial brilliance across the dark water.

I walked out to the end of the dock, to take my bearings and, truth be told, to check on the leak. To say there was nothing is, of course, to say rather that there was everything, intact, as it should have been. So that was how this worked. The moon rose from the state of Nevada. Wavelets broke on the stout wooden piers under me. Rocks gently rearranged themselves on shore, in sounds of clack-clacking low-tide pull. The water was clear. Blue.

And my own condition? It had been nearly three days by now and I seemed somehow not to have suffered any real symptoms of my abrupt, reckless discontinuation of otherwise perfectly helpful drug-taking by way of the test, the forced self-help gesture, cry for help, and embrace of bravery however unplanned or ill-conceived. I had saved the lake, saved myself, cause and correlation be damned. For my effort at going cold turkey I'd been given the unexpected opportunity, responsibility to do something even better, perhaps being cured or only obscuring my own little problem.

The size and scope of this sudden exaggeration of life, or its placebo effect, its vast ecological resonances, impossible proportions, the embarrassing implications of my own construction of it, the possibility that others out there, many, also had a natural unnatural collective disaster to confront, fire or flood or debris-flow, all of it held me there, wondering about further consequences. But not out of fear. More, I am forced to say, out of relief, curiosity, and affirmation. The night held me, as if without it I would just fall down. I let it.

Mr. Peck, the owner of the place, found me out there on the deck. I felt the solid vibrations of his footfalls before actually hearing or seeing him approach from the house. He actually seemed kind of pleased we were still all here, offering that it meant he wouldn't have to clean up, at least not tonight, ha ha. Peck was a big, barrel-chested healthy old fellow. He wore a crew-cut, suggesting he was ex-military. He put his arm on my shoulder, all avuncular-like, surprising me, not that anything could, really.

He looked around to make sure that we were alone, which we were, if only in the immediate sense, out on the dock. But there were, clearly, many more senses and many, many more people, witnesses, sensors I knew now.

"I heard from Myers, my neighbor," he said softly, nodding in the direction of the next mansion-dock up the bay, across the water, where that old man's bright yellow Zodiac hung now just over the side of the lake in its harness.

"What you did? Thanks for that, buddy," he said. "And you, not even being a local." He pulled his other hand out of his windbreaker and offered it. I shook it.

"You're welcome," I said. "Of course. Anybody would have," I said.

"No," he said. "Well, maybe. But that's not the way it works, actually. That was you, friend, all yours. Made to order."

"I take it there are others," I said. Or perhaps asked. "Have been?"

"Maybe one a month, typically. We've got it pretty well covered, as you can see. Preparedness, defensible space, a lot of old-timers who know the drill. Still, people dream up all kinds of new ones. Yours wasn't that original, frankly, though we don't get white that often."

He laughed. We both looked reflexively at the spot below us.

"We've had black and red, a lot, and, well, all kinds really. Sometimes the algae bloom confuses people. Green. Yellow. Nobody in particular is really responsible for that, thank goodness, and it's usually harmless though with global warming, who knows?"

"It really wasn't that hard," I said. "Once I saw it, recognized it. I knew what to do."

He nodded. Smiled. "Lucky you. Shallow water, too. That helps, believe you me," Peck said. "Honestly, you don't want to find something like that out in the very middle of the lake, where it's deep. And not much wider, either."

"The lake is 1,645 feet out at the very deepest spot," I recited.

"That's right, son," he said, smiling. "You read the material I left. Well done."

"I did, thanks."

"Somebody always does. We count on it, really. Big parties, sometimes two or three people in a group, sometimes they work together. You'd be surprised. It's in every house here on the lake. We make sure of that, let me tell ya."

"And somebody always acts?"

"So far," he said. "The thing is, ultimately, nobody ever gets one they can't handle. It's, well," he paused, "proportional. Just. Sometimes just barely. That doesn't happen much, generally, not in my experience, not in the rest of the world. But here, on our lake? Big man, big hole. Little man, little hole. Women, teenagers, too, but mostly men, it turns out."

"Yours?" I asked.

He laughed. "A long time ago. And, luckily, never twice, never again. It changes a person, as you can imagine."

"But in good ways, right?"

He seemed to consider an answer. "In all ways, I guess," he said. "Or, to be honest..."

I completed his sentence, thought, impossible assertion. Nobody else was going to say any of this out loud, not ever. "Because you changed it. You did. Let's be clear," I said.

He nodded. I hesitated, then tried to get it just right. "So I understand. You created, and then you transformed the circumstances. You intervened."

He smiled again, shook his head. "Okay. Yes. But I never said that, Otis. People would think I was crazy."

"And neither did I. Neither will I, not to anybody," I said. "Not ever."

"Right."

We turned together, away from the lake and the view of the distant, dimly outlined mountains, the moon slightly higher in the sky above us—above everybody, of course—now making its disinterested way across the entirely invisible and contrived boundary in the lake, a broken line a mile out, an absurd demarcation as nutty as anything, and as useless, and an idea as impossible as it could be.

"It's best that you don't. For everyone."

"Did I even have a choice?"

"Nobody knows, really," he said. "Probably not."

I heard the kids' laughter, the voices of Aris and Mrs. Peck inside.

"They used to call it the 'pathetic fallacy,'" I offered. "The Romantics, those crazy poets and painters. Sorry," I laughed. "I'm an English teacher."

"Right," said Bob Peck. "And nature abhors a vacuum. Like that. All nonsense, of course. Officially, anyway."

"Understood."

"But *we* know better…don't we?"

We walked back to the house, the otherwise precise and cooperative moonlight lost completely on the big artificially-illuminated glass doors of the house.

"So sorry about your father-in-law," he offered. "But Jeanie and I are so glad about the baby, of course. You are all such nice people."

Before we opened the sliding glass door and walked in, Mr. Peck turned to me, with one more question.

"And you? Did you get something out of the whole deal?"

And so we left the big house on the big blue lake, a day later than planned, all twelve of us. This time, driving home in daylight, the passengers included a healthy newborn, of course, as well as a brand-new adult lady orphan and one ex-junkie English teacher, the children having been instructed by circumstances, it seemed, on how best to welcome birth and to consider death, all the result of watching the adults talking, crying, driving, rowing, diving and embracing one another. What did anybody know that they had not learned exactly this way? We were given a big send-off by the Pecks, who offered us the place any time we liked.

Too young perhaps to make much of the details, Sophia explained that her uncle had plugged a leak, which was of course true. It seemed that all involved had been tested, each in their own way, been asked only what they could be expected to answer, and mostly had come through it. And everybody was rested, too, ready for school and work and whatever genocide might be remembered or denied.

Lincoln and Darwin did their homework on the long drive. Aris and I took turns at the wheel again, though his loving gaze at his child in the rear-view seemed to me to put us in some danger. Not that I was such an expert on assessing danger, or perhaps, indeed, I was exactly the best person to do that now! Either way, I took over the driving, my hands steady, my heart stronger, my eyes clear, sending him to the back to sit with wife and new baby and kids. Lizzy joined me, riding shotgun up in front until she fell asleep, into what anybody could see was a deep, restful into-body experience she so needed. We lacked a car seat for the infant, still unnamed, so the crew took turns holding her, which was probably illegal. I watched my speed and drove with the headlights on.

There was a christening to organize when we got home, a memorial service to arrange for Max. There were court appearances to complete for our misdemeanors, a new classroom full of students to greet, thank-you notes to write to those kind and wise and patient hospice nurses who'd cared for my father-in-law for so long.

I caught myself looking around to see if somebody was watching me, which had once meant watching me cheat or fail or obscure important details, the miserable behavior of low-grade shame and the recent habit of disappointment: an authority, a parent, a motorcycle cop waiting under an overpass up ahead, a doctor, somebody with a title there to confront me or, perhaps now, who knew, commend me? If there was a test, I was ready for it.

It was a weekday morning, after all, the long interstate mostly clear. Everybody else was back at it, in meetings or court hearings or classrooms or nursing homes or, yes, funeral homes. We'd soon be home ourselves, and maybe even beat the traffic into the basin which was only, when you thought about it, a day's drive from the famous deep, clear blue lake high in the mountains.

ACKNOWLEDGEMENTS

"The Neighborhood" appeared in *The Rattling Wall*.

"Accident" and "Storyboard" appeared in *Faultline: A Journal of Literary Arts*.

"Falling" appeared originally in *Ecotone*, then *Best American Nonrequired Reading 2013* and, finally, in *Ecotone*'s anniversary anthology, *Astoria to Zion: Twenty-Six Stories of Risk and Abandon from Ecotone's First Decade.*

"The Lady *and* the Tiger" appeared in *Orange Coast Review*.

"The Prisoner" and "My Denial" appeared in *Juked*.

Thank you!—Lisa Alvarez, Gustavo Arellano, Roy Bauer, Greg Bills, Michael Carlisle, Wayne and Deborah Clayton, Jonathan Cohen, Vivian Chu, Leslie Daniels, Keith Danner, Tagert Ellis, Vicki Forman, Kedric Francis, Michelle Franke, Federico Garcia, Ben George, Don Girard, Judith Grossman, Kate Haake, Grant Hier, Rhoda Huffey, Brett Hall Jones, Louis B. Jones, Jonathan Keeperman, Dawna Kemper, Jim Krusoe, Michelle Latiolais, Diane Lefer, Julia Lupton, Kat Lewin, Jim Mamer, Malcolm Margolin, Sue McIntire, Mia McIver, Bill Mohr, Bob Myers, Billy Ney, Naomi Okuyama, Victoria Patterson, Erik Rangno, Ryan Ridge, Tina Richards, Beth Riley, Sally Shore, Janice Shapiro, Grace Singh Smith, Marty Smith, Jeff Solomon, Honora St. Clair, Linda Sullivan, Jervey Tervalon, Louis Tonkovich, Georges Van Den Abbeele, Marilyn and Angelo Vassos, Oscar Villalon, Monona Wali, James Warner, Gayle Wattawa, Ming-Yea Wei, Richard Wirick, David Womack, Sandy Yang. And to my union comrades and friends at the Community of Writers.

ANDREW TONKOVICH'S essays, fiction and reviews have appeared in *Ecotone, Faultline, Juked, The Rattling Wall, Los Angeles Review of Books, Los Angeles Times*, and *Best American Nonrequired Reading*. He is the author of a novella collection, *The Dairy of Anne Frank*, and co-edited with Lisa Alvarez the first-ever literary anthology of his adopted county, *Orange County: A Literary Field Guide*. He edits the West Coast literary arts journal *Santa Monica Review* and hosts a weekly books show and podcast, *Bibliocracy Radio*, on KPFK (90.7 FM) in Southern California.

WHAT
BOOKS
PRESS

LOS ANGELES

WHATBOOKSPRESS.COM

CPSIA information can be obtained
at www.ICGtesting.com
Printed in the USA
BVHW031820290821
615542BV00005B/234